THE SOUTHERN HILL
AND THE LAND BEYOND

When a child was born to Mabel and
Hoe, just before lambing time, there
was great excitement among the creatures
of the land. Clusters of excited cotties
hung on the ivy round the window;
fleetings flapped about in the sky. The
tines, deep in the earth, had to be told
the news. For Little Hoe was to be one
of the people who knew about the land
and its king.

The people did not all share the
creatures' longing for the return of the
king and the restoring of the land. But
there were to be others who passed the
message on. There was Kerry, who managed
to befriend the westels, the sad, shy
creatures who were there one minute and
the next had become a dart of sunlight on
the water. And there was Esther who was
ill but who was like a creature of the hill
and the sky, a gentle piece of nature. Her
sister Morgen was to know, too – and to
take part in that glorious climax of all
things, up on the southern hill.

*This is an imaginative, rare and beautiful
book. Set in a gentle land of fields and
cottages, woods and rivers, it echoes
age-old themes of good and evil, spoiling
and saving, in a telling and evocative way.*

TO DAVID AND LOVELY AND THE MILK WONDER

The Southern Hill and the Land Beyond

PAULINE DAVIES

Illustrations by Rachel Beckingham

LION PUBLISHING

CONTENTS

One

KING GERALD'S GOLDEN BOX

There was a King Gerald, and he ruled over a land of ignorant and unruly people, and he loved those people even though they were ignorant and unruly, and ungrateful too. And these people, despite their foolishness, loved their king because he was so generous and kind, and they could remember no beginning to his reign, and they could imagine it having no end either, so powerful and wonderful did the king seem to them.

King Gerald's land stretched right across the southern hill, which is where the people lived, and the dark hill and the wild wood, where the waterfall was and where the king had his palace, and the great plain in the valley, and the distant places where the mountains were and the lakes and the sea. And in all the land, very wonderful creatures lived, as well as the people and animals, and they loved King Gerald and he was their king too.

In all King Gerald's land, there was one creature who did not love the king. The true form of this creature was too horrible to be looked upon, so it had acquired the secret of disguising itself. It could become invisible and ride on the storm. It could become lightning rushing out of the sky and striking down whatever it could, trying in all ways possible to ruin the king's land or to bring sadness, or to encourage the people to be more unruly in their behaviour, and more foolish. For this creature was the enemy of the king. And it longed, in a hopeless way, for the power of the king, and his wisdom as well.

Now King Gerald possessed a very special golden box, and it seemed to the creature that the power of the king and his wisdom were bound up in this box. For the box was a great mystery in all the land. King Gerald never appeared without it. Nor had any other creature been seen to touch it, or take it from the king. Nor did anyone know what it contained. And King Gerald would look into the box and he would smile, and whatever he saw pleased him greatly. So King Gerald's wicked enemy thought that the mysterious box contained the secret of the king's power, and perhaps even that power itself. And it bent all its cunning on taking the box away from the king and securing it for itself.

The creature's special pleasure was to disguise itself as a person and to mix among the people. In this form, the creature was known as Sylvester Sly. And in this form, Sylvester gained the confidence of Robin Raucous and Susan Sweetling.

Robin Raucous and Susan Sweetling lived on the very top of the southern hill. They were, of all people, the most foolish and rash and Sylvester saw this right away. They were ripe for his scheming and he succeeded in filling their heads with a desire that people in King Gerald's land had never known before, the desire for riches and power.

Now Sylvester devised a plan, and because he could not go into the presence of King Gerald without at once being recognized for what he really was, he sent Robin Raucous and Susan Sweetling in his place.

Robin Raucous was a great one for adventures and Sylvester filled his head with ideas of great battles against the king, with himself at the head of a victorious army. Victorious, because they had the golden box. And Susan Sweetling was vain and greedy, and Sylvester told her that when they had defeated the king, she would be queen, and she would be the most beautiful person ever, because she had the golden box, and all creatures would come thronging to her to hear her wisdom, because she had the golden box.

So Robin and Susan packed up their things and put on their best clothes and went down from the southern hill where they lived, to King Gerald. And when they stood in his great palace in the wild wood by the waterfall and the crossing streams, and when they were afraid to come before him, they remembered what Sylvester had said, and it gave them fresh courage.

But when King Gerald appeared before them, Sylvester's plan was all but forgotten. For Robin Raucous and Susan Sweetling had never before known anything like the presence of the king, and there was much bowing and obeyance-making and trembling, and they could not remember at all why they had come, and then when they did remember, they could not find voices in their throats with which to say the words they had come to say. King Gerald waited very patiently for them, and they struggled hard, and then Robin began.

'You have a golden box,' he said, and he tried to sound casual and in command of himself. He made some sort of a gesture at the box, which King Gerald held in his two hands in front of him. 'That box there.' He was finding it very difficult to take his eyes off the box, and very difficult to gather his thoughts together, and quite impossible to lift his gaze up a little and into the face of the king. 'The box that only you know anything about ...' He trailed off into silence, and then he realized that he had not finished at all, there was a lot still to be said, and then he started again.

'Well, you see,' he said, 'the people have asked us to come and see you about it, haven't they, Susan?'

Susan nearly fainted. She twitched in her best clothing and gulped and breathed big breaths very slowly and managed to get the words 'Oh yes' out of her mouth, and then she blushed to the roots of her hair and kept her head right down in case King Gerald should read in her face that she was not telling the truth.

Robin kept going hoarse and he blushed as well and then he went white, but all things taken into consideration he managed much better than Susan. He managed a whole big speech, all in one go, peppered with coughs and splutters, but quite without forgetting his words or forgetting why they had come, or anything else. It went something like this:

'Well, yes, like I say, the people have sent us. Yes. Um. They feel that you have betrayed them because you keep the contents of your golden box a secret from them. Yes. They don't like secrets in such a good and wonderful land. No. They think that maybe you don't love them because

9

you keep secrets from them. They want you to show that you love them. Well, I mean, they want you to give us the golden box so we can show it to them and they'll know that you trust them and there'll be no more secrets any more. No. Not even this one little silly secret.'

It was a pretty poor speech, a mixture of Sylvester's eloquence and Robin's lack of it. But the general sense of what Sylvester wanted was there, and it was an enormous effort on Robin's part. He gulped down the end of it and for some time King Gerald said nothing at all, and both Robin and Susan twitched in their clothing and sweated a good deal and thought they were found out, they must be found out, and that if the king didn't say something soon, they would pass out with fear.

King Gerald was very sad indeed. He was wise and he knew that Robin had not been telling the truth. He knew too that it was the creature, Sylvester Sly, who was at the back of it all. The speech bore the marks of Sylvester upon it. And King Gerald knew how much Sylvester wanted the golden box for himself. At last he spoke.

'If you were to see the contents of this box of mine,' he said, 'I am afraid you would not understand. Great wickedness has come into your hearts and you must realize wickedness is a blinding thing. It is something that blinds your minds and takes away your understanding. I can see a greed for power and authority behind everything you have said. Be sure and remember this. My power does not lie inside the golden box. The secret of the golden box is another thing. Rather than containing my power, the golden box contains a sign of that power.'

Robin and Susan were quite amazed by these words, and they could not at all understand what the king meant.

'This is not the time for you to understand,' said King Gerald. 'At the right time, all my people will understand and there will be no secret of the golden box. But there will be no wickedness in that time. As long as you continue in your present ways, you never will understand the secret of the golden box, you silly, vain people.'

Then King Gerald did an amazing thing. He said, 'Come with me,' and he took Robin Raucous and Susan Sweetling, who were shaking more than ever before, right through his palace and he brought them out on to a terrace overlooking the crossing of the streams, and he sat them down under a lovely tree and he brought food and drink to them.

'You plot against me,' he said, 'but I want you to be my friends. I want you to have all good things. But if I give you a good thing at the wrong time, you will not enjoy it. So you must wait for my time.'

Robin and Susan just sweated and twitched more than ever. They sat on the terrace, red-faced and quite confused and trying to be polite, and they attempted to eat the food that the king offered them, but it stuck in their throats. Then they attempted to drink his good wine, but that stuck in their throats too.

King Gerald smiled. 'I give you the finest wine in the land and you can't drink it,' he said, 'and I give you the best of my food and you can't eat it.'

Then he became quite serious with them again. 'Wickedness has choked my good gifts in your throats,' he said. 'I can give no good thing to you while wickedness remains. Throw off the wickedness. You will enjoy nothing at all till you do!'

Robin Raucous and Susan Sweetling sat very still and were quite sure that the king was going to punish them now for their wickedness. But King Gerald said, 'Eat, if you can, for the journey back home is a long one,' and 'Remember all that I've said. Remember it always.' And he left them alone on the terrace.

Now when they were sure they were alone, Robin and Susan jumped over the terrace and into the wild wood and with warnings about wickedness ringing inside their heads, they climbed very fast, up the wood and away from the palace of the king. They were sure that King Gerald would send servants to follow them and punish them.

The trees in the wild wood knew of their fear and their wickedness and played little games with them, tangling them up and getting them lost, and soon all their best clothes were quite spoiled and they were crying and scared and alone in what seemed like a terrible place. But at last

they came home, and the king had sent no servants to punish them and only the trees had played with them and they were back on the southern hill and were safe. And when they got home, Sylvester was there.

He made up the fire because they were shaking so much, with fear and with cold, and he sat them down by it and made them say everything that had taken place. They repeated it all, and they repeated the words of King Gerald as exactly as they could, and they were still filled with bewilderment over all that he said, and the things that he did.

Sylvester sat some way apart from the fire. Not being an ignorant person at all, but another creature altogether, he understood more clearly what King Gerald had meant, but he did not understand in full or else he would have given up his plotting and his wicked schemes. Instead, he encouraged Robin and Susan to rest and find plenty to do and try to forget all about King Gerald, partly because he knew that in their present state they were of no use to him, and partly because he needed the time to make a new plan.

Sylvester left Robin Raucous and Susan Sweetling by the fire in their home. He went down through the wild wood and up on the other side to the dark hill and he stayed in the dark hill and thought about what was to be done.

Now Sylvester was so wicked a creature he could not see truth when it was presented to him. So he still believed, despite all that King Gerald had said, that the golden box contained the secret of the king's power, if not the power of the king itself. He could not stop thinking about the box and how it would bring great things to him. And so he made a new plan whereby Robin and Susan would steal the golden box from King Gerald and give it to him, and then he would claim everything that had been the king's for himself.

Robin and Susan needed a lot of persuasion, a lot of promising, and, more effective in the end, a lot of threatening, before they would consider going back again to the palace of the king. They tried to make Sylvester understand that King Gerald knew things, and that it would not be possible to get the box from him because he would know that they were coming. But Sylvester thought himself too subtle for King Gerald. And he certainly was too subtle for Robin and Susan, for he succeeded in winning them round and sending them off with detailed instructions as to what they must do and how they must go about it.

So the two foolish people went back again to the king's palace in the wild wood between the wheat hills and the orchards. But this time it was night. And while King Gerald lay in his royal bed, they stole the golden box from his side. They were very frightened. Nobody but King Gerald had ever touched the golden box. And it had never been removed from the king's presence. They were quite unsure of what would happen. Indeed, Sylvester himself had been unsure of what would happen when he had insisted that it was not possible for him to come with them on their little mission.

Susan pushed Robin forward because he was supposed to be the lover of adventures. In the sleeping presence of the king, Robin had as much trouble with his feet as he had had with his voice when the king was awake. It took quite a while before he could make them work, and then when he got them to work and got right to the box, his hands played him up, and he had to stand right over King Gerald, who could well wake up at any time, and wait until they got going again in order to pick up the box.

But when he eventually managed to pick it up, nothing at all out of the ordinary took place. The king did not awake, and the box did not explode its magic all over him, and everything seemed just as before. So Robin backed off from the royal bed and rejoined Susan Sweetling, and together they crept, trembling quite considerably, away from the palace and back through the dreadful wild wood and home to the southern hill where they were to meet with Sylvester.

Once away from the palace, safe and with nobody following them, they stopped trembling and became quite excited, for they were sure that between them they had what was in fact the power that made King Gerald everything that he was.

They were very foolish. King Gerald watched their departure with his golden box through eyes that were closed as though he was asleep. He didn't need to open his eyes to see that his box was being taken away, and he was very sad. But he too made plans, much better plans than Sylvester Sly's, for all the creature's cunning. And it was part of his plan that the enemies should be allowed to take the box, just as he knew that they would not understand what they found, and it was part of his plan that the unruly people, and the wicked creature too, should find out just how powerful he was, and what his power was like in its full glory.

The king called one of his messengers to him and ordered that it should follow the foolish people and watch over them all the time that they had the golden box. When the messenger had gone, he lay back in his royal bed and closed his eyes again and was very sad at the disloyalty and deceitfulness that had come into his people.

These very people, on the other hand, were extremely excited by now. They took the box along the wheat fields and up along the grazing land and back home, where Sylvester was waiting for them. All three were filled with the sweet and terrible longing for power. Sylvester learnt at once that Robin and Susan had absolutely no intention of handing the box over to him, and it took much cunning and talking and making himself nice and promising many things, before he could even get them to agree to give him some share in whatever the box contained.

'Well, come on then,' said Robin Raucous at last. 'Let's stop talking about it and get on and open it up. I want to see what King Gerald keeps in this box of his, after all the trouble we've had getting it!'

But Sylvester, not being a person, was not so impatient. Sylvester was shrewd. He thought of things that silly, ignorant people would never have considered. Like, supposing there was some magic inside the box and when they opened it up they would all be destroyed and then nobody would have the power and the riches and the wisdom of the king ...

'I think we should just keep the box as it is,' he said, much to the surprise of the others, and with some difficulty too, for he had longed for the golden box and was as curious about it as the people. 'After all, the fact that we've got the

15

box will be enough to make people follow us instead of the king.'

'That won't do,' said Susan Sweetling, and the desire for power had sharpened her wits. 'I mean, who's to know then that this is *the* golden box, and not any old golden thing? If King Gerald knows what's inside and we don't, nobody will believe us at all and the king will still have all the power and everything.'

Sylvester was angry at himself for letting a stupid person think of something that he hadn't thought about, and he took his anger out on Susan by saying that in that case, perhaps she should be the first person to look inside, and then if it was safe, Robin could look inside, and then if it was still safe, he, Sylvester, would look. That way, if there was some magic in the box, they wouldn't all be lost to it.

But the others weren't having any of that! And the three of them fell to arguing about who would open the box first. They were an ugly lot, squabbling together, while King Gerald's golden box sat in the middle of them all, pure and lovely like the king himself.

And while they squabbled, the king's messenger stood in a dark corner, its glory wrapped about in shadows, and it took careful notice of everything that they said, and it was prepared for action of any kind, depending on what they decided to do.

Finally, because nothing else could be agreed upon, it was decided that each of the three should lay one finger across the lid of the box and that they should all pull it back together and each look in at the same moment, on the count of three.

They laid their fingers on the box, and looked, with little love or bravery, across it and at each other. This time there was no fighting about anything. Each of them knew that to hold back from this task meant losing the power of the box to the others. Even Sylvester was unable to think of a good reason why he should stay back until he knew if it was safe to look, and still hope to share in the treasure.

If there was a treasure, of course. They could be releasing a terrible power. Or a magical creature that the king kept shut away because it was too dangerous to be let out. What awful thing would they find inside the box, and what would it do to them?

Slowly, the three fingers lifted up the golden lid. Slowly, they removed their fingers, the wicked ones, and they stared again into each other's faces. Susan Sweetling began to count.

'One.'

A little perspiration dripped down Robin's nose.

'Two.'

Although she was counting, Susan had forgotten all about how much she wanted to be a queen.

'Three.'

Sylvester Sly was trying to work out a quick way of turning into a worm and wriggling away, should the worst come to the worst, when he thought he saw something move towards them from out of the corner of the room.

But it was too late to do anything. As one, the foolish people and the wicked creature looked into the king's golden box.

Then they were drawn into the box. It happened very quickly. They were aware of the walls of the box around them and themselves very small and the room where they had been very big and then the lid came down and the room where they had been had gone and it all was so quick it was hard to believe, and they didn't feel strange, it was so quick.

They found themselves, amazed and bewildered, in another place. They were in a bright, long valley, steeply sloped on either side with hills upon which the sun shone brightly. The slopes of the hills were covered, lower down with trees, and higher up with wheat, and it seemed, from the colour of the wheat, that the time was near for harvesting.

They found themselves standing in a little dip, with swift, clear streams cutting through the ground all around them. Also surrounding them were lovely, graceful trees, heavy with leaves of all colours and shapes, and out of the earth grew long, soft grasses, tender as though people had never walked across them.

They looked, and they were confused by what they saw.

This was not a new and strange land. They were not sure what it was, but all of it, from the shape of the hills to the sound of the streams, was familiar, and not in a general sense, but in a very definite way, as though they were standing in some well known but long forgotten place, but a place that had become so fresh and lovely that it was impossible to recognize any more.

Each thought this thing privately and was afraid to say it aloud, for each wondered if this feeling was part of the enchantment of the golden box, and each was full of fear.

Then Sylvester Sly looked into the faces of Robin Raucous and Susan Sweetling and he knew that they were thinking the same as himself.

'It's true,' he said. 'We know this place. We must have been here before, but when or how, I don't know yet.' And he bent all his powers on trying to unfathom this new mystery.

Robin Raucous and Susan Sweetling just walked about and looked at everything. They tried shutting their eyes and listening, in case the sounds that they heard were familiar. The sounds were very familiar, but neither of them could work out why.

Susan Sweetling walked some little way from Sylvester and Robin. She looked all around her, at the deep, swift streams which crossed over each other as they rushed down the valley, and up at the hills covered with wheat ready for harvesting, and she knew where she was, and it was all even more of a mystery than before. She called back to the others.

'I know where we are,' she said. 'Robin, you should know. When we were here before it was night and we couldn't see so much but we could hear the streams in the ground. And before that, we had battled with the trees,' she said, 'and we were glad to get back to the wheat fields and the grazing land.'

The others came to where she stood.

'This is the palace of King Gerald,' she said, and she indicated with her arms all around her, and she was very pale and her voice was full of awe and amazement. 'This is King Gerald's land.'

Sylvester Sly and Robin Raucous struggled with this idea. It was true! They were standing where the king's palace ought to be, but the ground around them was as they had never known it before, it was a pure thing. And there was no sign of a palace. It was as though they were at the very beginning of everything and the land was quite new.

Susan, thinking about the freshness of everything, and trying to understand it all, and quite unable to do so, bent down and ran her hands through the soft, tender grass. As she did so, the grass creased up and turned brown. She jumped up at once, and backwards, and she knocked into the others, and they all stared at the withered grass and couldn't understand what Susan had done.

And when they turned round and looked back to where they had come from, they were greeted by the sight of great desolation. For everything that they had touched, everywhere that they had walked, had turned brown and shrivelled up and the little valley was quite spoiled.

'We're spoiling it,' cried Robin Raucous in great horror. 'Everything we touch, we're spoiling!'

While Robin and Susan stood quite still and were afraid to move as much as another inch in any direction, Sylvester Sly, the creature who was not a person at all, drew apart from them. He had some hard thinking to do. He remembered all those things that King Gerald had told the people about his box. 'At the right time I'll show my golden box to all my subjects,' he had said, 'and they will understand. But in that time there will be no wickedness and unruliness.'

Sylvester was on the very edge of unfathomable mysteries. He struggled to understand things, but he could not. One thing he did know. His time in this place could well be limited, according to whatever King Gerald had planned to do, and the land was perfect and new and ripe for all the mischief that he could possibly pour out on to it. Sylvester Sly determined to act very quickly indeed.

But other things were happening. In the shadow of a tree, the king's messenger watched the confusion as Robin and Susan tried to decide what to do and to understand what had happened. In a second, he turned himself into a great, white bird, and made a commotion, flapping about in the leaves and branches of a tree and floating into the sky.

Robin and Susan turned round at once because this was the first sound of life other than their own that they had heard. They saw the bird, and together they looked up into the sky to watch its flight.

The lid of the sky was bright blue. Written across in King Gerald's own hand was this message:

TAKE CARE: THIS BOX IS THE PROPERTY OF KING GERALD

Robin cried out and Susan almost wept. They turned round, as one, to pour blame on to Sylvester Sly who had first prompted them to steal the golden box, but the place where Sylvester had been was quite empty. He had disappeared.

Robin cried out again, and Susan fell on to the ground. And where she fell, all the grass turned brown.

Two

LITTLE HOE AND THE
CREATURES OF THE LAND

These things concern the sadness among the creatures that was turned to joy. For these things are about the spoiling of the land and how it was saved.

The great book of the tines, the wise creatures who once lived on the land but were driven into the darkness, told of these things. It said that the land had one great lord, and that the lord was King Gerald. It said that there were two kinds of creature in the land, the old creatures and those who had come newly into the land.

The old creatures were the tines themselves, and the westels who were the water creatures, and the cotties who lived on the land in the places of greatest danger, and the fleetings who were the messengers of the air and passed between the king and his creatures and one creature and another.

The new creatures were the people. The great book of the tines did not say how the people came into the land, but it recounted everything that took place from that time. For the people were the spoilers of the land, and it was they who drove the tines underground and they who made the land a sorrowful place for the old creatures to live in. For whatever they touched, where it had been good, it became bad, and where it had been fresh, it became stale, and where it had been rich it became poor.

The old creatures of the land met together in a very great gathering. The tines read out the old stories of the land, and they all remembered how things had been before the people, how good the land was and how King Gerald had been constantly among them. And they remembered how happy they had been together. But now there was no happiness and King Gerald had gone away and the land had been spoiled and the people lived in it as though they were lords, and the old creatures lived in fear because of the people's destruction.

Then all the old creatures talked together and they decided to send the fleetings to find King Gerald and to ask him to come back and help them in their trouble. For surely King Gerald would want to stop the spoiling of the land. And surely he would want to save his old friends from their present trouble.

So the fleetings went off, in search of King Gerald who had once been so often among them all. They went high through the sky and for a very long time and it seemed that they'd never find the king and they almost despaired. But at last, far from their land and the places they knew, they came upon the king's palace. And King Gerald came and greeted them and took them into the palace, and they told him all their troubles and their news.

King Gerald was very loving and very gentle with the creatures. 'This is a great mystery,' he said to them. 'I have not forgotten you. I have not forgotten my land. There is a dreadful creature in my land, an old enemy, and he has blinded the people to what they are doing and he has taken away their past so that they have forgotten me and think that they are lords of the land. This is a very dreadful thing! But I have a plan. At a special time, I will come back into the land and I will take the land for myself again. And when I do that, it will become lovelier even than before, and perfect. And in that time, the enemy will be punished for ever. And in that time too, you will be very glad, because you have endured terrible things, and they will be over for ever.'

The fleetings were full of excitement when they heard this thing, that King Gerald had a plan, and when they learnt that King Gerald had not forgotten about them and about the land. But they were frightened as well, because of the dreadful enemy and because of the terrible things that they were to endure.

'Now listen carefully,' said King Gerald, and he drew the fleetings around him gently. 'I want it to be possible for the people to be glad, just as you will be glad. I want to give them back their history, and the other thing too that the wicked enemy has taken from them, their love of the land.'

The fleetings thought this not a good idea at all. They hated the people, you see, and did not relish the thought of sharing one little bit of the gladness to come with them.

'You must see,' said King Gerald, 'that to make things known to the people is to give them the love that they do not possess for the land, and then if they love the land they will become your friends and will wait with you for the time when I come.'

'And you must see too,' said the king, 'that to bring gladness to the people is to defeat the wicked one. He knows that I love the people, and he tries to steal them away. I cannot let him take what I have chosen for himself! Oh no, at the end of this present time, they shall be glad, just like you, and the enemy shall have lost them.'

Then the fleetings could see that it was good to make all things known to the people and to snatch them away from the enemy of the king and to have them for friends.

'But how can these things be?' they said. 'The people are so wicked and dreadful in all that they do, they could never see what we see and know the things that we know.'

'When the time has come,' said King Gerald, 'I will tell you that too. And until that time, you must wait and be brave.'

So the fleetings left the presence of the king and returned to the land and they told the other creatures what the king had said and all the creatures hid away from the people because they did not yet love the good land, and they waited for King Gerald to make more of his secret plan known.

The tines, the wise ones, went deeper into the earth, and they took their wisdom with them and they did not go about on the land any more. The shy water people, the westels, sailed right out into the ocean and the deep swift rivers and the bottomless lakes and went down into them, deeply like the tines, and they cried and were sad, and as the tines carried the wisdom of the land, they carried its sorrow with them.

The fleetings, who were the sky people, and the messengers among the creatures, kept to the sky. At nights, they rested on clouds or high mountain tops. Sometimes they came down to the old creatures, but they were frightened and nervous. The days when they came and joined in with the festivities of the land seemed over. Indeed, it seemed that the festivities were altogether over.

And the other creatures, the little earth creatures, the cotties, lived all around the people, in the fields and trees and hills, and they hated the people because theirs was the greatest danger, and they were the brave ones who fought against the spoiling of the land. Theirs was a desperate battle to save the little things, flowers and leaves and insects and animals, from the dreadful spoiling to which all things were subjected by the wicked and foolish people.

Seasons passed and old people died and new people were born and grew up and had children. The enemy of the king was the same as ever, and so were the old creatures in the land, because death and age were special to the people. And King Gerald was the same too.

One day, he called the fleetings to his palace. 'It is time for you to know more about my plan for the people,' said King Gerald. 'You will remember that I am going to make it possible for the people to love the land as you love it, and wait, as you wait, for me to come and take back the land, and I am going to make it possible for them to be glad in that day, just as you will be glad.'

The fleetings remembered these things.

'I have chosen a person,' said King Gerald, 'who will know all the things that you know, and see all that you can see. He is soon to be born. You old creatures will have the task of instructing him in all that you know and showing him all that you can see.

'When he knows what you know and sees what you can see,' said King Gerald, 'he will become like a father to my chosen people among the people. From out of his knowing the things that you know and his passing on of these things, will come those who will be like his children, like a family, my special people in all of the land. They will love the land and they will teach a caring for the land to the other people.

And they will endure, as you endure, until I come to make gladness among you all. And then they will be glad, even as you are glad, and they will be very special among all creatures, for they will be my loved ones.'

Then King Gerald gave the fleetings some very detailed instructions about what the old creatures of the land were to do, and who was to do what, and when they should do it.

The fleetings went away, excited about the unfolding of the plan, and they told the cotties and the westels what King Gerald had said, and the westels told them where they might find the tines, and they went into the mouth of the dark caves and called to the tines, but they would not go deeply into the caves because they were creatures of the air and the sunlight, and they were too afraid of the darkness. The tines came and stood some way apart and listened to their special tasks in King Gerald's plan, and then all of the old creatures knew, and they all waited.

One early morning, just before lambing time on the land, Mabel and Hoe succeeded in producing a child. Not an unusual event in itself. Ever since people had been in the land, they had been producing children, and when they grew up, the children had been producing children.

But whereas it was usual for the old creatures in the land to groan each time another baby person was added to the many, on this occasion, clusters of excited cotties clung on to the ivy that grew around the old attic window, and fleetings flapped about in the sky, and all the old creatures were very excited indeed.

The leaders of the cotties were the keepers of King Gerald's Oak, the most perfect tree in the land, and they had pride of place round the window and they saw all there was to be seen, and very worked up about it they became too.

'Go and tell the westels and tines,' they said to the fleetings. 'Go quickly and tell the tines to start working. This is the person. This is the one that King Gerald told us about!'

The fleetings lifted into the sky and sped across the land and they found the westels and tines and told them that the person had been born. The westels cried for all the old creatures, because this thing had come about, but it was the cry of solemn joy, and the tines, deep in the earth, began to weave away with their wisdom, a power that surrounded the baby boy like a strong net, and they began to prepare for him, and to prepare him, too, for the part that he was to play in King Gerald's plan.

Little Hoe sat up in bed in the middle of the night, quite awake, and startled because the feeling was coming again and he didn't know what to do. It was a sweet feeling. It began somewhere down his back and it crept all over his body and he would fight it and then it would be too strong because although in the early days it had been weak, it was stronger each time and now it was a mighty feeling. And then it would be all over his body and it would take him, take him off...

But where did it take him? He would be in the other place and the other place seemed so familiar and nice too, and he would be quite at home and yet he would never completely lose the sense of being in his bed and in the long room where he slept with mother and father with the animals stalled downstairs underneath them all. And he would be there, in both places, all at the same time. He would surface from the feeling, struggling to hold on to it or at least to remember it and remember the creatures that he met in it. He would wish that he could have lost himself in it and forgotten all about who he was and where he really was too.

Then he would feel very sick and would start crying, or sometimes even shouting, and he would be afraid because he couldn't understand it at all.

Mabel came rushing across the long room. She hardly slept any more because of Little Hoe's strange stories and his screams and shouts and tears. She would lie awake, waiting for him to cry and worrying about him and wondering if it ran in either of their families, hers or Hoe's, this strangeness about the child, and what she should do.

'It was much bigger this time,' Little Hoe told her. 'I feel sick! I don't like it, I don't want it to happen again. Really, I don't!'

But he wasn't too sure about whether he wanted it to happen again or not. For each time that it happened, he gave himself up to it more willingly, and it was only in the panic when he first woke up with it creeping over him, and then afterwards when he tried to work out what had happened, that he didn't like it or want it to happen again. While it was actually with him, it was wonderful and he wanted it to go on and on.

Mabel got water for him and said nice things and stayed with him until he had fallen asleep. Then she crept down the long room and back to bed and she woke up Old Hoe and told him all about it, as she did every night.

'I know you think I'm silly,' she said. 'But there's something terribly wrong with him, terribly wrong.'

Little Hoe woke up and it was as though his blood was on fire. He wasn't afraid of the place or the feeling that was coming over him at all, and he gladly let it take him. Lovely feeling! Warm and tingling and powerful! And lovely place! He wanted the lovely place. Everything in him strained to be in the lovely place and with the nice people there and everything in him fought to keep the real world, the long room and father and mother and the animals downstairs, right out of things. And when he came out of it, he fought like a mad one to stay there and to hold it all and to remember it so that if ever in the real world he was there, he would remember and recognize it all.

And then it was gone and forgotten again. Little Hoe lay down in his bed and didn't cry at all. It would come again tomorrow night and it would be stronger. One night he would never come out of that lovely place.

Little Hoe sat up in bed. It was a very dark night, quite without a moon. Except that it wasn't at all dark in the other place. Gracefully and with ease, he slipped into it, sunlight and sweetness and kind, lovely faces of the other creatures all around him, and they were his new friends and there was nothing to fight, no coming back to battle against. He had come through to stay.

In the morning, when Mabel awoke in the long room,

Little Hoe's bed was slept in but empty, and Little Hoe had gone.

An ancient tine came down along the edges of the ploughed fields and across the lambing and the calving pastures and through the orchards and down into the valley. He was tall and proud and from his bearing you would not have known how the bright land and its sun made him suffer. It was a long time now since he had gone under the earth and into the dark.

Cotties of the land saw him go by and were thrilled because they knew that the important thing was happening, just as King Gerald had said and that the ancient tine was obeying special instructions from the king himself.

Fleetings of the air passed overhead and spread themselves out in all their glory, to shelter him from the bright morning sun, and he strode on, leaving great footprints behind him on the ploughed field and scattering sheep before him in the pastures, and he was glad that the fleetings were there over his head, taking care of him, and leaving him free to bend all his efforts on performing the work of the king.

He came to the steep little valley and the woods above the streams and the waterfall, and he strode down through the bracken with impatient steps. After some time, the valley grew thicker with trees. He began to look around, choosing first one path, then another, then none at all. The path faded away into light and shade, birdsong and silence.

'My friends,' the ancient tine called to the trees. 'I have come to perform the task given me by King Gerald, to open the eyes of the people. To let them know things that they do not know and see things that they cannot see. Let me through, I beg of you.'

There was a stirring in the wild wood, and then the trees, who like all things in the land were subject to King Gerald's wishes, parted for the great tine, and bowed down before the one who had come to do the king's will.

But there was a tree that did not bow down before King Gerald's servant and did not part to one or other side in order to let him through. Knotted and gnarled, it stood right in the ancient tine's pathway, and whichever way he took, its great branches tangled him up and tried to strangle him or to sweep him off the ground and hang him up in the air.

The old tine drew back and looked hard at the tree and looked hard at all the other trees. And because he was a tine, and wiser than other creatures, he saw something in the tree that was not in the other trees. He saw two bright eyes in the tree, cold, wicked eyes staring at him, and he knew quite surely why this tree was not obedient to the servant of the king, as were the other trees.

'You are no tree,' said the old tine. 'You are the creature with the terrible form who can change itself into many things. I know you, you wicked thing!'

And he took a great stick from the ground and tried to drill it into the eyes of the tree, because the eyes were a soft place while all else was hard, and because the eyes were like the centre of the thing.

The tree suddenly disappeared. The path was clear for the tine to step down along. The old tine stood with his stick wavering in the air and no enemy before it. He dropped his stick with the shock of it all and spun round, half-expecting some foul trick to come upon him from behind. But the tree was quite gone and the wicked enemy of King Gerald had passed on to do other deeds. The tine trembled for what might yet come between them both. He picked up his old stick, gathered himself together and passed, hesitantly at first but then with greater confidence, along through the trees.

He came down beside the stream and looked about him and could not find what he had come out of the dark places for. He searched for some time, down by the water. At last a young westel came and stood before him, gleaming with stream water.

'We have no reason to love the wicked people or to wish good upon them,' it said. 'But we love King Gerald and he loves them, and so we do his will. Come with me, and hurry, and I will show you where the child is being kept.'

The young westel took the straight old tine by the hand and led him through the stream for some long while. As they journeyed together, it told of a great wave that had gathered in the stream and rushed along it and almost drowned the child at the place where he was being kept.

'Surely there is evil around us,' said the westel. 'For no good thing in King Gerald's land would try to destroy this first of many people.'

The ancient tine was sure that this too was one of the forms of the wicked enemy, and he told the westel about the tree with the eyes in it, and they knew that they should hurry even more because the enemy could be close at hand and wherever it might be, it was sure to be planning harm for the child and the end of King Gerald's plan.

And so they came through to the pool beneath the waterfall, and there, caught up in the thicket that grew all around, quite safe, unscratched and in a deep sleep, lay the child, Little Hoe, for whom the ancient tine had come out into the bright land above the earth.

Westels are shy creatures, the shyest of all King Gerald's creatures. Only for a very grave matter would a westel have taken a tine through the waters. And now that this task was completed, the young westel went back into the stream, without a word, and became a dart of sunlight, and was gone.

The ancient tine stepped out towards the thicket, across the pool. He stepped out as the chosen messenger of the king. He stepped out to take the child, the first of the many.

As he did so, a great sheet of fire flared up between himself and the child. The tine knew at once that this was another of the forms of the enemy. And of all forms, this, the last barrier between the old tine and the child, was the most subtle. For the tine, the creature of the dark places under the earth, was dazzled by the brightness of the flames and his eyes were full of the pain of it and he could not look into the fire and his strength was of little use to him, for it seemed that he was almost blind and there was little that he could do.

He struggled through the pool, one hand over his eyes, crying out aloud, and he tried to scoop water into the flames with his free hand. But the flames just got higher. Then he tried to make his way around the fire, but the flames just followed him and they danced right in front of him, whichever way he turned, and there was no getting away from them. His eyes stung and watered and as the flames danced before him he could see that the fire too had eyes, wicked, burning eyes, and they watched him and laughed at his suffering. They were the eyes of the enemy of the king, and they spoke to him.

'You are defeated,' they said. 'In the moment of your glory, I have defeated you!' And the eyes of the fire burned into the eyes of the tine, and they laughed all the more.

Then a great anger came upon the old tine, for it seemed to him that nothing could defeat King Gerald if he had made a special plan, and that the wicked creature's cause was impossible and already lost, and that he had the power to defeat anything that stood up against the king. He was the champion of King Gerald! And as he thought this thing, the pain went out of his eyes and he could look straight at the wicked fire, and he felt strength in his body and he was not afraid and he was not at all defeated. This was the moment of his glory.

'King Gerald has chosen the child,' he said in a great voice. 'He has chosen me to care for him. And I shall care for him!'

And he threw himself into the fire and set about attacking the flames, all the time driving into their centre, the eyes of the wicked enemy of the king. As he fought, it seemed that he was the mightiest creature ever, so strong and powerful was he. The flames began to scream out and the eyes no longer laughed and the fire began to crease up about its eyes, trying to protect them. The old tine continued to beat away at the eyes. There was a new sound in his ears, a sound of comfort and encouragement, a strong sound, and he crushed the eyes and the flames screamed their final scream and fled.

The new sound in the old tine's ears was the song of the westels, the song of victory, sung deep in the streams and the lakes and the ocean. All the king's old friends in the land had seen the great battle, wherever they had been, and there was not one who had not given everything to encourage the old tine. He stood where the fire had been and listened to the song, the strangest sound in all the land, and he heard the whispers of the trees and the encouragement of all things. The air was clear again and he could hear birdsong. It was fresh, the clear air, and it smelt now as though there never had been an evil fire. The tine's eyes no longer smarted and stung with the pain of the fire, and he was perfectly healed.

He stooped over the thicket and gently untangled the young boy. The child stirred not at all. It was as though his state was deeper than sleep. The tine held the child against himself to keep him safe. He looked about and decided which path to take, and the trees bowed down all about him and made the path clear for him. One hand clasping the child, and guiding himself with the other, the ancient tine began the climb up to the pastures.

It was evening by the time that he reached the fields where the cattle and the sheep had been. The old tine strode on, straight and strong and with the chosen child in his arms and glad for the coming darkness, across the land and up to the hills and towards the dark caves where the lessons were to begin.

Three

THE HERMIT AND THE WOMAN

There were two hills and they faced each other with the wild wood between. Above were the great hills where the caves were, and below lay the great valley, and beyond were other places, mountains and lakes and the ocean, but these places were a long way off, and the two hills and the wild wood and the valley were at the centre of the land.

One hill was very barren and very cold and the wind up there was sharp and high and few people lived on this hill, for it was like a tree struck by lightning, dead and scarred. The other hill was rich of soil and wheat grew on it and there were orchards too, and higher up was pasture land where the animals grazed. It was a gentle, abundant place, and when people from the valley looked up at it they thought that it was the finest thing they had ever seen.

And it was here that the Hermit Hoe had made his home. He planted crops on the hill and he reaped and stored, and he kept animals for milk and food and to carry him about, and for friendship too. And he had a little wooden dwelling-place with tiny windows and a tiny door and shutters to keep out the weather and a stout stone chimney, and here he lived with his animals too.

Now in this place, the Hermit pressed and crushed all sorts of flowers from the pastures and the wild wood and pieces of tree, and he made dyes with these things and with these dyes he made pictures upon his wooden walls.

And he made books too, of thick, hard stuff, quite unlike what we know as paper, and wrote in these books with big, heavy characters, all the great secrets that he knew, from the way the land grew, to names and types of dances and little pieces of music that he had learnt from the cotties, for until these times, people in the land knew nothing about music and dancing and how to make festivities.

The Hermit made poultices too, special mixtures with pungent, strange smells, and when he was sick or when his animals were sick and sometimes even when the trees and the things that grew around were sick, he would administer these poultices and cure the sickness with them.

And because of all these activities, people drew apart from the Hermit and he was alone. For you must understand that until the time of the Hermit, there had been none of these things in the land, no music and dancing and no making of books and writing things in them and no making of pictures and no curing of sickness either. So the Hermit and his activities were regarded with great suspicion, and if people had to journey across the hill, it would be up at the top of the pasture, and as far from him as possible. So he lived beyond the company of people, on his side of the hill.

One night, there was a great storm on the hills, wind and rain and all the trees creaking about and the animals restless and nervous. In the morning, the Hermit came out of his wooden dwelling-place and set to work, gathering in branches that had fallen from the trees and storing them for firewood, and repairing the fences round where the animals were kept in the day, and generally setting things in order.

He had long, white hair which was tied behind his head in a big knot, and a long white beard, also tied in a knot, hanging over his chest. His skin was brown and thick and folded over itself many times, like the bark of a very old tree. You could hardly see his features, for all the folding of his skin. His mouth you might only have seen if he had opened it, and his nose not at all, and his eyes were two pricks of light and you had to look very hard to find them. They were like a new substance among all the knotting and folding over and wrinkling of the rest of him. They were very sad eyes. All the time and no matter what he was doing, they were sad.

To see him so, working as he was, you might have had some idea why the people in the valley thought that he was not a person like themselves and why they were afraid of coming close by where he lived. But you would have seen, too, how wrong they were to be afraid of him, for he moved about all the time with love and tenderness, gentle with the animals as he led them out of their dwelling-place and to where the fences had been mended, tender with the trees as he lifted the bowing branches and tied them back as they had been before the storm. And no dreadful person as the old man was thought to be could possess love as he possessed it and gentleness as he possessed that as well. He went round everywhere, putting all things to rights, his hands lingering over the young and fragile things that had been torn down by the storm, his eyes full of sadness that they could be spoiled.

By noon, the repairs had been made and the old man sat on a large, flat stone in front of the little door and took a stone jar and drank cider from it and looked all about him. Beyond the damson trees and up at the top of the pasture, a few sheep passed between earth and sky and disappeared on the other side of the hill. Down in the valley, people moved about, and above them all in the sky, little clouds drifted casually along. It was the soft, gentle day that comes after the rough storm. The animals in their enclosure snuffled about, grunting or whinnying according to their kind. The Hermit sat still and quiet, and looked upon all that was to be seen.

He began to cry. You would not have heard him cry, nor would you have seen tears on his cheeks, but if you had looked quite closely you might have seen how bright his eyes had become; they were like little springs of water and the tears were little, fast streams that disappeared straight away into the deep folding over of his tough old skin. And he stayed like this, still and quiet and crying, right into the afternoon. Not once did he cease his crying, nor did he move.

A cottie came along the pasture where the sheep had been and along the ditches and the hedges and between the damson trees and right up to the Hermit's dwelling-place and to the doorway and the big flat stone where the Hermit was sitting. He got right up beside him and put his little cottie arms around him, for love and encouragement, and cried with him. 'Poor Hoe,' he cried. 'Poor Hermit Hoe, poor Hoe.'

And when he had cried, the cottie took the Hermit's jar of cider and drank from it and passed it to the Hermit. And he drank from the stone jar too and stopped his crying and smiled to see his little friend, but he was still very sad.

When he saw that the Hermit was smiling, the cottie laughed and jumped up and said that he would do a dance, and he did a dance, and played his instrument while he danced, by way of accompaniment, and he said that the Hermit should go and fetch his own instrument and join in with him.

But the Hermit did not enjoy seeing the dance or hearing the music. When the cottie wanted him to join in he said that these things belonged to the time when he was young and he was old now and the time had come for other things.

The cottie said that there was always time for dancing and music, but because he could not make the old man happy with these things and because it was so sad to dance alone, he stopped his dance and came round by the Hermit and they cried again.

Then the cottie said that this was a very bad thing, that they were crying all the time. And he began to tell tales to the Hermit in order to bring him encouragement.

He told the tale of how the creatures had seen him when he was born, and how excited they all had been because he was going to be a special person in the land. He told the tale of how the great tine had fought in the wild wood to protect the Hermit Hoe and how the wicked enemy of the king had been blinded for all time by the great old tine. And he loved to tell this tale for it had been a very great battle. He repeated little secrets that creatures count as nothing but people would think very great and strange, to encourage the Hermit in his wonder at the land and the way it was made. He even said that perhaps they could go on a journey to all the places where the Hermit had been when he was young and the pupil of the tines. Then he could remember those great old days.

But the sadness was upon the old man and he said no,

those places could not be returned to, time could not be turned back, and he would not look at the little cottie, and for a long time they sat in this way, silent and staring off at the valley.

Then the Hermit spoke. 'I know things that other people do not know,' he said. 'I know about the land and I love it as other people cannot love it, and I know how we began in the land and how we shall end. And I know about the king, and I know how to be glad for what will come at the end of the present time, and glad in the land now, for its goodness. I have been glad in my life too, even though I am a person and a spoiler of the land. For I have learnt to cure and to be gentle and to love. I have had much gladness. But in these times, the gladness has gone out of me and I have become very old and very sad too.'

'When I was very young,' said the Hermit Hoe, 'it was promised me by the king that I would be like the father of a great family of people who would know what I know and enjoy what I enjoy. Even death would not make us sad, for we would all be waiting, in life or death, for the time when the king would come back to the land and make it good again and make us good again too.

'I have waited all my life for these people who would be like my family. And my gladness in the land has become empty for they have not come and I know what I know, and it cannot be shared.

'I still wait,' said the Hermit. 'I am an old man and I still wait. Soon I will die, for we are spoilers in the land and we die. And there is no family. None have come to me to learn from me and to be like my little children, seeing what I see and knowing the things that I know. I will die and everything will be taken with me into death. I alone will wake up in the day when the king comes back into the land. But I will not be glad, as you will be glad. I will have failed in what I should have done.'

These were the words of the Hermit Hoe. As he said them he got up from his stone and began to pace about between the damson trees, and when he had finished, he leaned up against one of them and seemed to fade into it so that it was just one great, brown, knotted-over mass of growing stuff, and he covered his bright eyes over with his hands and despair was great upon him.

The cottie was very distressed. 'You must remember what you have been taught,' he said. 'You are a special person. You are our friend. You are the first of the people to be the friend of the creatures and we shall have many friends among people after you and because of you.'

But the Hermit did not hear the words of the little cottie, and the cottie went away sadly and told the other creatures of the great despair that had come upon the first of the special people of the king, and then they were all sad.

After the cottie had been gone some long time, the Hermit saw that the day was beginning to draw into evening and he began to gather up his tools and to start leading the animals back to the dwelling-place in readiness for the night. His movements were tired now and he shuffled with an old man's shuffle and you could see the weariness about him with everything of life.

Just at dusk, when the shadows were beginning to draw out under the damson trees and as the old man was getting the wood inside in order to make the fire, a fleeting came out of the sky and right between the trees. The fleeting stood before the Hermit and the Hermit stood before the fleeting and he marvelled at the glory of the creature, as he always marvelled when he saw a fleeting, and then the creature spoke to him.

'You are waiting for the good time of the king,' it said. 'We all wait for the time of the king. And that time is not known to us. King Gerald knows that you are old and that you are sad. But he says you must wait. His time will come.'

Then the fleeting touched the face of the Hermit with its wing, very gently, and the Hermit lost all his weariness and he knew that the time would come and he would be like a father to many. And tenderness came back into him, and he was comforted.

The fleeting went away from him and left him thinking about these things. Then he saw that the night was coming very close and there was still no fire and still many things to do, and he picked up his wood and stooped and entered the dwelling-place and joined the animals there. He began to make up the fire and to set about feeding them all.

While these things went on inside the Hermit's dwelling-place, out in the land, a woman was picking her way through the orchards and the fields of wheat and the grazing land. She was a strong, stout woman, in her middle years, wrapped all about in warm stuff, and her head covered with a headdress and her face flat and quite blank and round, shining like a full moon and showing neither tiredness nor excitement, and she climbed, never wearying in her journey, and was soon upon the dwelling-place of the Hermit and at his door.

She thundered a strong fist down upon the wood. The Hermit, from inside, called to know who was there, but he made no motion towards letting her in.

'A woman is here,' said the woman. And she stared at the wooden door and the wooden door stared back at her, each as expressionless as the other.

'What do you want?' said the Hermit. He lifted back a shutter and saw a mound of woven stuff around a body and a head with a headdress wrapped around it and a big, round, shining face sticking out underneath and showing nothing at all.

'I want to see the Hermit,' said the woman.

The Hermit got away from the window because he was afraid of being seen and he was not used to people coming to his door and his heart beat inside him and he didn't know what to make of this at all.

'What do you want with the Hermit?' he said. 'Tell me that, eh.'

The woman stirred herself not at all. She just continued staring at the wood of the door and her eyes said nothing.

'Let me in,' she said. 'If you have secrets about life and death, let me in. And if not, I will go away again.'

Then was the Hermit Hoe moved by her words and he came to the door and opened it, and his heart beat greatly inside of him and a new feeling was upon him, and the woman entered his dwelling-place.

But he hardly saw her, for behind her and between the damson trees were the cotties that lived on the land, and many fleetings too, and he heard far away the song of the westels and he knew that this was a special time and that all things were combined to bring him encouragement in what he had to do.

The woman came right into his dwelling-place, past where the animals were stalled and the fire, and to the dark place by the wall, and there she removed her headdress and he could see that she was an ordinary woman of the land and a shy one too. He came up to the fire and sat there in its light and looked at her and she looked all about her, at the secrets that he kept in his dwelling-place and the strange pictures and the instruments for making music.

'Tell me why you came,' said the Hermit very gently.

She turned all her shy, unmoved attention to him and she stared at him with her big, flat, round face, and when she spoke it was very shyly and quietly.

'I was married very young,' she said. 'Very young, you must understand. I bore my husband twelve children. All of them died. I have seen twelve births and twelve deaths.

'Then, because there were feelings inside of me that I couldn't understand, I left my husband. I travelled about in the land and saw many things. I saw the sea and the mountains and great forests, like I had never seen forests before. But I always had the strange feelings inside of me and my travels didn't take them away and they didn't help me to understand them. So I went back home to my husband and he took me back to him. I live with him now and I will live with him until he dies and then I will have known thirteen deaths. And then I will die.'

'Tell me about your strange feelings then,' said the Hermit, very gently.

'They concern birth and death,' said the woman of the land. 'Birth I have seen to be such a little thing in the land, and death too. I have thought life cannot be all birth and death. The beginning of life must be more than birth, and the end more than death. Life is a very big thing. Birth and death I have felt to be small. I came to you to find if you knew about the beginning of things and the end, and to see if you would tell me these things. For my feelings are very strong, and they trouble me greatly.'

So the woman of the land finished speaking, and as she

finished, she stared blankly as ever at the Hermit Hoe. She was just a simple, plain-speaking woman. But the Hermit could see too that she was wise and that she was a special person, and he was full of the encouragement of the creatures around him, and he was a person with new and wonderful things to tell.

So he began his telling, and he told as the tines had told him. His story was of the richness of the land and of its spoiling. It was the story of the king of the land and of first things and last ones too. It was a story of great gladness.

As he spoke, he brought down his books and read from them, and he drew pictures with his finger in the ground round the fire and his voice grew strong and proud, for all his life he had waited to tell this story to this strong, shy woman of the land.

The woman nodded and listened and when the telling was completed, she said quite simply, 'These things are about the beginning and the end. They are greater than birth and death. You are the only person who knows what is greater than birth and death. And now I know too.'

Then the Hermit Hoe and the woman of the land put their arms around each other and cried together, and the Hermit said, 'You are my child, you are my daughter,' and the woman of the land understood and the blankness left her face and she became glad, as the old man was glad.

Then the Hermit Hoe took her to the doorway of his little dwelling-place and showed her the creatures, the cotties and the fleetings, between the damson trees. The woman saw the creatures and she heard too what the Hermit could hear, the song of the westels, the encouragement from distant places. The Hermit said, 'These are the friends of the king, and they are our friends too,' and he brought the woman out to the creatures.

So the creatures made a feast, and the Hermit and the cotties taught the woman of the land how to dance and how to make music, and together they all taught her how to be happy and how to rejoice. And so they all danced and sang and were happy and rejoiced, all through the night until morning, and then the Hermit took the woman of the land aside and said that he had many great lessons to teach to her.

After this, for many days, the Hermit Hoe went about with the woman of the land, teaching her from his books and conducting her on journeys to places of great importance, and he taught her about the land and how to live in it, and about King Gerald and what a king he was for the people to love, and about the things to come, until her lessons were complete.

Then, one morning, the Hermit made her get ready to go back into the valley. He gave her his books and his pictures and his instruments for making music and said that she must be very careful and remember everything that he had taught her. And if she needed help, she must count on the creatures, for they were her friends now, and would always be there for her encouragement.

'You must take these things to the people,' said the Hermit. 'I am going to die and only you of all people possess my knowledge and my burden is passed on to you.'

'Why must you die?' said the woman. 'You are most special of all people to the king. Surely you will not die!'

'We all die,' said the Hermit. 'Because we all are people.'

He took the woman out onto the pasture and he said that he would come down the hillside with her, for safe-keeping. But the woman was very sad, and she said no, if they would not meet again in the present times, this was the place to say goodbye.

'I will stand here then,' said the Hermit, 'and watch you go. And I will not see you again until the king comes and all things are made good and as they should be.'

The woman took the gifts, the books and the instruments and the little pictures, and put them inside the folds of her big, wide clothing. She stood on the pasture, wrapping the headdress about her big, round face and the Hermit Hoe and the woman of the land kissed each other goodbye and the woman turned her face away, and then went down through the pasture and the fields of wheat and the orchards while the old man watched her going until she was no more to be seen. Then he knew that the love of the land and the enjoyment of it and the caring for it had been taken among the people, and the love of the king of the land, and the knowledge of the past and the things to come too.

When she had quite gone, the Hermit went back to his dwelling-place and said goodbye to all his animals and all the little creatures. And when he was quite alone, he prepared himself to die.

And you must not think this was a very sad thing. For the Hermit Hoe had seen the working of the king in the land and he knew of the goodness to come, and he was very glad.

Four

KERRY AND THE WESTELS

The enjoyment of the land and the understanding of the good things in it were not the rights of people from the beginning of time, but were like a wonderful gift that had been passed down through the generations. King Gerald had given the gift and he had given it through the little creatures in the land. But the people did not know about King Gerald, nor did they know about the creatures, and they accepted the good things as though they had always been there. Only a few people knew where they came from, and these were the strange people.

Kerry was a boy much like any other in the place where he lived. He enjoyed the good land and he enjoyed the goodness of life, and this, because he was very young, was all dancing and singing and walking the girls about and fighting and drinking good, rough cider and going out all night and putting his old mother in an absolute fit of worry about him.

But he knew what his mother and his father and his brother Dan and the other people in the place where he lived did not know, that the enjoyment of the land and the understanding of things in it were not the rights of the people. He knew about King Gerald and about the creatures too. He knew that in past times people had known nothing in the land and he knew that they were spoilers of the land and destroyed wherever they touched. So he loved the little healing things that he had learned and that had been passed down, all the more, and he loved the land all the more and the good things in it, and he counted it a great privilege to know what he knew and to enjoy what he enjoyed too.

Kerry's old mother thought that, if anything, there was too much enjoyment in his life. It was always drinking and fighting and walking out with the girls that he was about, and it was never helping in the house and doing chores and learning how to do the work that a man ought to do. And when people suggested that there was something rather unusual about young Kerry and told stories about how sometimes there were strange people in the land who said strange things, Kerry's mother said, 'Oh no, not Kerry, he's too lazy to do anything but enjoy himself,' for Kerry wasn't like the strange people, oh no, he was too good-for-nothing to be like that!

She would scold Kerry for his laziness and Kerry would just pat her on the head or laugh, and sometimes he would say that he wasn't at all lazy, he spent his days learning about things she would never have dreamed about, or else he would walk away and say nothing at all.

Kerry's great friends were the fleetings. He went on travels with them because he wanted to see everything that there was to be seen and to know everything too. He told this to his mother, and she threw a nervous hysteric and he never told anybody else.

He tried to tell her other things too. He came into the kitchen where she was baking one day and sat beside the fire, right where he was most in her way, and he told her that he had another family, that he was part of another sort of family, and they were made up of all very special people.

She dropped her baking all over the floor and shouted at him to be quiet and she went quite red in the face and was very cross and wouldn't let him finish what he wanted to say and wouldn't let him explain what he meant either, and she told him that he must never say such a thing ever again, and especially not outside the family. Then she went rushing out of the kitchen, crying noisily as was her way, because her son was a strange person after all, and she wondered if it was her fault or father's or even if Dan had anything to do with it.

But she wouldn't talk about it and she wouldn't let Kerry talk about it. She just worried to herself from that time onwards and wondered always what he was thinking now, and never dared ask.

Kerry, quite undaunted by his silly old mother, just got on with enjoying himself. He took a girl out walking in the fields one day and he tried to tell her about some of the places he had seen, in order to impress her. But she thought that he couldn't possibly have seen what he said he'd seen, and she was frightened by the things that he said and the fields were a long way from home and she just turned round and ran away.

He gave up walking with girls and spent his time drinking with the boys instead. They would take their jars of cider and go and lie in the orchards, which were empty and quiet at night, and they would fight and tell tales. But when Kerry began to boast of where he had been and what he had done, they just thought he was drunk and they took him right home to his mother and left him with her and she was very cross indeed. But Kerry wasn't drunk at all. And from that time, he resolved not to mention the places he had been and the things that he knew any more, and he knew that people wouldn't believe the things that he said, just because he chose to say them.

So Kerry became quieter. His mother cherished hopes of him finding some work to do, but instead of that, he went out more on his own and he wouldn't say, when he returned, where he had been or what he had been doing.

The truth was that Kerry found life in the place where he lived very boring. He liked the good things, the fun and the fights, but the times in between were intolerable and he wanted life to be all excitement and adventure and fun, and so he went about more and more with the fleetings and he sought out things to do that had never been done before, and he wanted more than anything to be the first in some great thing.

One day, the fleetings had some reason for going to the westels, and Kerry, who couldn't bear to miss out on any single thing that happened in the land, begged to go along with them to the place where the westels might be found.

They were on the southern hill. The fleetings were hanging about in the trees and being very relaxed and casual and Kerry was lying on his back, smoking a clay pipe and staring up at them and at the bright blue sky too, and feeling quite pleased with himself as he usually did.

But the fleetings seemed to think that this wasn't such a good idea, that Kerry should come too, and they fussed about and talked among themselves and in the end they came to Kerry and said that didn't he think it would be a good idea if he went home and got himself some sort of work to do there and placated his old mother? And they said that they thought perhaps he was spending too much time with them, going about with them and sitting around with them and smoking his pipe and nothing else.

This took Kerry quite by surprise and he didn't like the idea at all. He would have expected his mother to complain about him because she didn't know what he was doing all day long and because she was stupid and her opinion was stupid and he cared nothing for it at all.

But he thought a lot of his friends the fleetings, and of their opinions too, and they knew that he was working very hard just by being with them. Learning things was what he was doing, and so he was quite hurt by what they had said and he jumped up and told them so and told them too that he was very busy, far too busy to go home and find other work to do, because he was preparing his mind for the great work of his life, which was yet to come.

The fleetings didn't think that Kerry was preparing his mind for the great work of his life at all. They thought that he was finding life a much pleasanter thing, going about with them and having adventures and seeing things he never would have seen in the normal way, than he would have found it at home, planting potatoes and helping to keep them all fed.

But they knew as well that he was young and excited with all of life and that he would hunger after adventures until that time when he came up against things that couldn't be understood or dealt with, and they knew that such times would deal hardly with him and they could see already the hard times coming close, so they were gentle with Kerry and never again sent him home in this way. And they took him with them to the westels, as he had wanted.

So Kerry got to see the water creatures. A fleeting took

him up in its wings and the company, a dozen or so of them, flew down the southern hill and across the valley and to a lovely river bank, and there they came to rest. The fleetings made Kerry get behind a tree and told him to be quiet and not move, for the westels were very shy creatures and the fleetings said that they hated people above all other things, and if they knew that a person was there, they wouldn't come out of the water at all.

Kerry stood behind the tree and tried to be quiet and still and the westels came up out of the river and the fleetings spoke with them.

But then Kerry got all excited because they were so different from anything else he had seen and so lovely too, and he fell out from behind the tree and the westels went back into the water, quick and like sunlight fading as a cloud comes, and they would not return.

The fleetings were very cross with Kerry and they took him away and told him not to come and see them again until he had learned to control himself better.

Kerry stayed at home for three whole days, and he succeeded in amazing his family and his mother as he began to make plans for jobs that he could do along with his brother Dan. But then he felt the call of the water creatures and he was off again to see his old friends, the fleetings.

Kerry loved the rivers and the lakes. He had been to the sea once with the fleetings and had never wanted to return from it, and the idea of creatures being in such places was quite splendid to him. He got back to the fleetings and hastily told them that he had learned now the way to control himself very well indeed, and then he wanted to know about the westels.

So the fleetings told him about them. They said that they were very sad creatures, for they carried the sorrow of all the creatures in the land upon them. And they said that they were very shy and that they hated people, as Kerry should know. They said too that even among the creatures they were shy and no other creature could claim friendship with them and they were hardly ever to be seen and were as mysterious even as the deep places in which they lived. They said that the westels had a great beauty, and Kerry remembered what he had seen of them and knew this to be so, and that they were the lonely ones for they were the ones without friends in all of the land.

'Oh,' said Kerry, sensing an adventure in all of this. 'Then I shall be their friend. Will you take me back to the place where they live?'

The fleetings tried to explain that westels wouldn't accept Kerry's friendship just because he chose to offer it, but Kerry was all insistent and excited and he counted nothing more important any more than that he should know the westels. The harder the fleetings tried to explain about them, the more he was sure that he could be their friend. For he very much wanted to be the first in something, he wanted to do what had never been done before.

Finally, the fleetings agreed to take him back to the place where the westels had been and they agreed to call to the westels that a person had come and wanted to be their friend and he was one of the special people in the land, the chosen of King Gerald and he was not to be feared. Then, they said, there was nothing else they could do. For if the westels didn't want the friendship of people, nothing at all would make them accept it.

So the company of fleetings took Kerry with them and flew down the southern hill again and along the valley and to the lovely river and then they brought Kerry down on to its bank. They stood on the bank with trees all about and the fleetings went to the edge of the river and they called out that a person was here, one of the great family of the king's own people, and this person would like to be the friend of the westels.

Nothing happened at all, and the fleetings said to Kerry that nothing would happen either, but that they would go right away and leave him to his own devices and one of them said that it would come back later in the day and see how he had got on, and take him back home.

Kerry stood on the bank of the lovely river for some time and then he began to walk about and to plan what he should do.

The creatures were shy, he thought to himself. So it was important not to alarm them. He began to talk to them, supposing that they were there of course, and to talk very quietly too, and in what he considered to be his most unalarming voice.

He told them all about the colourful and exciting person that he was and all about the wonderful adventures that he had had and how *all* the creatures were his friends and how they could be too. And he expected them to come rushing out of the water, almost as soon as the words had rolled off his tongue, and then they would have great times together.

But nothing happened. The westels didn't come rushing out of the water at all. They didn't even bother to surface to see who was there. Kerry called out a bit louder to them to please come and he said how much he wanted to meet them and how he wanted to be their friend. But they still didn't come and he only succeeded in chasing away a few silly birds in the trees and a few old squirrels, and he stood by the river, feeling rather foolish and as if he was talking to himself, and didn't quite know what to do.

He thought that this was going to be a long business after all and he was going to have to be patient. He sat down and was very still indeed and very quiet, and he thought that if he sat long enough, the westels would probably come, just to see if he had gone, and then he would leap out and introduce himself and win them over with his engaging way, and then the great times would begin.

But the westels didn't come out of the water and Kerry just got very stiff and very cross and after a long time of staying still, which was much against his nature, he jumped up and shouted, 'You silly old westels, I don't want to hurt you. I don't want to do anything bad. Why can't you come and be friends with me like the fleetings are friends with me?'

As he said this and as he jumped up and down on the river bank and as he got red in the face and made his throat sore for shouting so hard, a fleeting came out of the sky and down beside him.

The fleeting told him that shouting at westels wouldn't do at all. He'd never get to be friends with them like that. It suggested too, ever so gently, that perhaps the westels didn't want to be friends with Kerry and it even went as far as to suggest that they couldn't be blamed, perhaps Kerry's opinion of himself was a little too high in the way that he described himself to them. But Kerry got very cross and said that the fleeting had no business listening to what he said to the westels and he said that the westels weren't in the river anyhow, the fleetings had brought him to the wrong place.

'Not so,' said the fleeting calmly, 'can't you hear the westels singing?'

Kerry listened, and as the wind blew one way he thought that perhaps he could hear something, and as it blew the other he thought that he could not. But the fleeting insisted that the westels were here, they were deep in the water, and they were singing.

'All right then,' said Kerry, who still wanted to do things that had never been done before. 'If the westels are here, then I shall be here too. I'll keep coming back and in the end we shall be friends, and I don't care how long I have to wait, we shall be friends.'

The fleeting took Kerry back home and he saw for himself the way to the river from the place where he lived, and from that time on, he went to the river alone and many times, and sometimes he talked to the westels and sometimes he was silent, all the time trying to find the way in which he might win their friendship.

A change came over Kerry at this time, and the fleetings noticed the change and they thought that perhaps he was growing up and his mother noticed it too and she began to hope that it meant the beginning of new things, and perhaps he would work like Dan and father worked, and perhaps he was growing out of his silly ideas.

For Kerry was mellowing. He was growing out of his silly ideas, but not in the way that mother had hoped, and he was growing into new ones.

When he was by the river and talking about his great adventures, repeating them over and over again for there were not many of them, he remembered what the fleeting had said, that his opinion of himself was too high, and they seemed like empty adventures and hollow words, and he came to be ashamed to talk of them, and then his days by the river were spent in silence.

And when he spent silent days by the river, hoping that perhaps a westel would come, he thought about what they were like and why they were shy and he realized that he hadn't cared at all for the westels in the beginning, and he hadn't thought these things before, about what they were like, because his only interest in them was to be their friend when nobody else had been their friend, and to achieve something that had never been done before. And he thought this an empty reason to seek out new friends, and was ashamed of himself for this too.

And as he spent his days by the river, Kerry learnt what the real desire for friendship was like. He thought much about the westels, how shy they must be and how gentle and he loved them without seeing them and he waited with a patience that was altogether new to him and he thought that perhaps one day he could count it his privilege to see them or speak to them. And if they would not accept the friendship he offered, he would go right away and not return for that would be their privilege as well.

He talked about new things to the westels. He told them about mother and father and about Dan too, and he said that Dan was the most horrible person he knew, and he talked about all the silly little things that occurred in the place where he lived. He talked about people and what they were like and what he was like and how he had changed and how much he had learned, and each day that he came he brought a new story of some simple little thing that had taken place, and he chatted, just as though they were there. He even tried floating bits of food on the water as offerings of goodwill to the westels. But his offerings of goodwill seemed as unsuccessful as everything else was proving to be.

Summer blew itself out into autumn and that in turn into winter. Still Kerry made the journey to the river as often as he could. Mother clucked over him and said that it was dreadful, the way he behaved, and Dan tried to follow him sometimes. But Kerry ignored mother, as much as that was possible, and he got rid of Dan quite easily, for he knew the land much better than his brother who had never gone far from the place where they lived. And he told himself that he wasn't a child any more, oh no, he was old enough to do just as he liked and mother and Dan would have no part in it.

One night it snowed. In the morning, the land was covered all over and was thick and white.

Kerry's mother was stoking up the fire and fussing about trying to get the kitchen warmed and Kerry came through, dressed up in all his heavy old winter clothing, and she threw down the poker right by the fire, and said, 'Oh Kerry, you surely can't be going out today?'

Kerry said that he could be going out today, in fact he was going out today. And he went out and he left mother to retrieve her poker and get on with her jobs and compare him, as usual, with other mothers' sons in the land and with Dan, and he got back down to the river and pushed all these silly things out of his head and thought about the westels.

He half expected to find the river frozen over, but it wasn't at all. He crouched down over the white ground and began his usual chatter, and as he talked he just got colder and colder and then the bright sky clouded over and before long, big flakes of fresh snow began to fall.

Kerry just went on talking. At first, he tried to shake the snow off as it fell on to him and while he talked. But the snow got faster and soon it quite covered his head and all over his body, and so he got up and began to stamp about and blow on his fingers and still he kept talking, all sorts of nonsense.

And then it happened, quickly and unexpectedly, for Kerry had quite got used to the idea that the westels just didn't appear. A creature came out of the water. It came right up to him and he stood very still and couldn't believe that it was a westel and that such a thing could happen. It was slender and light and very shy, and it was all movement, quickly beside him and quickly gone too, so that he was not sure if it had really been there.

But he found that he was covered in some sort of big garment, when the creature had gone, made of green, soft stuff and unlike any substance he'd seen before, and he wasn't cold any more and he wasn't wet from the snow and he was all wrapped about in the green stuff, warm and dry.

He rushed to the edge of the river and peered through the snow falling fast into it and could see nothing at all. And he stayed by the river all day and he talked and talked, but the creature didn't return. Then he went back home, in the warm and the dry, and he hid the green thing in his place for secret things and went on inside and amazed everyone, much to his delight, because he was so dry and unweathered.

After that, he went to the fleetings and they said, 'Oh well, it was snowing,' and, 'Were you sure it was a westel and not an extra-size snowflake?' and they made little jokes out of it and teased Kerry, because after all westels wouldn't come to people. But Kerry produced his green thing, and they stopped teasing him and became very serious, and they said yes, it must have been a westel, this was westel stuff all right, and Kerry was very excited that such a thing should have happened, and started to jump around and shout and he felt he might burst, he was so happy.

But the fleetings were still very serious. They said that Kerry was favoured as no other person had been, and they warned him to take care. Kerry could not understand this warning. He thought to question it, but he was in too excited a state. And soon after, he forgot about it altogether.

He went many times back to the river, more even than before. Sometimes he stayed overnight, and he took his green stuff with him and was warm and dry and when he came home his old mother examined him for morning dew and when she could find none, she swore that he was up to something, and who had he been with and what was he about, and why was he not wet, like a young man would normally be wet who had stayed out all night?

Spring came and Kerry had not seen the westels again. Summer came, and one morning Kerry went down to the river, and he found that the westels had come. They sat on the far side of the river and looked at him and would say nothing at all.

Kerry sat down on his side of the river and his eyes were full of them. He sat upon his garment of green stuff and just stared. They were lovely. They were smaller than people and slight and almost transparent, but not quite so. And they were like children, with the faces and expressions of children and the beauty of children. He began to talk to them in a very quiet voice, afraid that he would make them go away, but they didn't go away, they remained quiet and still and let him talk on, just as he talked every time, and when he had finished his talking, they went back into the river without saying a word.

Later, when he came to the river, they were there again. They listened to what he had to say and then, as before, when he had quite finished they went back into the water, silently. This happened many times.

One day, Kerry took cakes from his old mother and he laid the cakes on the water as a present for the westels, and they took the cakes and passed them around and poked at them and then played with them among themselves, and laughed at them. Kerry explained that they were food, and the westels didn't seem to understand so he took a cake from his own portion and ate it and said that it was good, and then the westels stopped playing and laughing and ate the cakes and said that they were good too, imitating his little movements and the tone of his voice, like children in this as in all other things.

The next time that he came, the westels laid things upon the water for him, fine garments of the green stuff and a stone, polished and shining and of many colours, and a little bag of the most wonderful sand that shone in his hand as though it had been made of powdered gold.

Kerry took these things home with him and hid them in the secret place and treasured them. And from that time he was the friend of the westels. It was a shy and simple friendship, and it was good. It was the best thing that Kerry had ever known and he spent all his time by the river and was hardly ever home. Mother saw that the change in him was complete and it wasn't as she had hoped and when he did come back home, she moaned and she cursed at him and he just went away again.

When Kerry had gone one day, she called to Dan from out among the cabbages and she told Dan to find where Kerry had gone because Kerry wouldn't say and something was wrong with him, and Dan said not to worry, he'd find

out, and mother was glad for her Dan, because Kerry was useless and strange and it was good to have one son who did as she told him.

So Kerry just lived by the river. The westels taught him new things, and they were secrets that he treasured as much as the bright stone and the fine sand. They took him into the water with them, and they showed him the land beneath the surface of the river, and a lovely place it was too. And he watched them and all the time he marvelled at them for they were so delicate and so much like children who have never been hurt and so tender, and they made tenderness come out of him and gentleness and wonder too, and he just didn't know himself any more.

'Why do you let me come with you?' he said to them once, but they wouldn't answer him, they just showed him some new thing, and then later they said, 'You are our friend. We love you.' And they cried, and Kerry cried and he had learnt new and wonderful things about sorrow that people had never known before.

One day, Kerry sat by the river with the westels around him and they said, 'Build a house here and find work to do.' And Kerry explained, much as he had explained to the fleetings, that he was working, he was learning things, and the westels were sad and said that he wasn't working, he was just enjoying life, and enjoying life was good, but if he loved the land as they knew that he did, he would work on it, taking care of it.

This was a new idea altogether to Kerry and he thought about it and the westels said that they would still be his friends. He should find a wife and have some children, and they would be friends with his children and his children's children too. For the family of Kerry would be loved by them always. But they said that it was wrong for Kerry to be so apart from the land and the people. He should work. He should have a wife. That was how people should be. And Kerry went away from the westels and back to his home and he said that he wanted to be on his own and to think about things.

It was while he was home that the dreadful thing happened. And when the dreadful thing happened, Kerry remembered his old friends, the fleetings, and the warning they'd given that he should take care.

He awoke feeling strange. He felt something wrong and he thought that he heard the westels crying to him, then he thought he did not. It was late in the morning and quite light, but Kerry went back to sleep and tried to forget the strange way that he'd felt. But he woke again, feeling strange again, and he was sure that the westels were crying.

He decided that he must go down to the river, and go at once. He dressed very quickly, and when he was dressed he went out to the secret place where his treasures were hidden in order to take the green stuff, as was his custom, to the river with him.

He found the garments of green stuff, folded over in their place, just as before. He found the old birds' eggs and the feathers and the things of his boyhood, just as they'd always been. But the beautiful, finely polished, coloured stone which he had been given by the westels and the little bag of fine sand like powered gold had both disappeared.

Kerry took everything out of the secret place. He turned everything over. He searched all around the secret place in case they had fallen out. But the treasures weren't there. They had been taken.

Kerry rushed into the house with the most dreadful look right across his face. His old mother saw the look as soon as he came in and she went quite white, then she went quite red and for a moment the two of them just stared at each other. Then she turned round very sharply and tried to rush out of the room and Kerry knew quite surely that his treasures had been stolen and that she was involved in the theft.

He grabbed hold of her before she could get away and he began to shake her very hard, all the time with the dreadful look right across his face. She began to cry in a silly, loud, gulping way, but Kerry could hear the mournful cry of the westels, and he knew that his mother's tears were nothing at all to do with real sorrow and that they were just a vain and foolish striving after pity. And he felt no pity for her. He was just thinking all the time of the westels and afraid of whatever had taken place and afraid because they were crying and he felt so strange inside of himself. And he was very harsh and he made his old mother tell him where the treasures had gone. At first, she would say nothing, and Kerry shook her hard. Then she set up her crying, the loudest so far, and Kerry just shook her more. And then, in the end, mother said Dan had taken them and they were very great things and they were going to be rich soon because Dan knew where Kerry went and where the treasure came from and he'd gone there and he was going to dig up the river and soon there'd be treasure for them all, her and father and Dan, and not just for Kerry.

She accused Kerry of selfishness, keeping the treasure to himself, and she said no wonder he didn't work and that was what he had been getting up to, and Kerry just shook her all the more in his rage and he said that they wouldn't find treasure to make them all rich, his little things had been gifts and he hadn't dug them up from the river at all. He went down there for much more important things, and being rich wasn't important at all.

His mother answered back with more grievances against him and Kerry just pushed her away and he rushed off from her.

He went down to the river, as fast as he could. And as he got nearer, the crying of the westels got louder and his head was filled with it and he cried too, as the creatures cried, because it was through him, and through all his vanity in winning their friendship, that harm had come upon them and he thought that their beauty would be taken away and their loveliness spoiled.

He came down to the river. Never had he seen such a sight. Dan stood right out in the river and he had been digging it up. He had made little dams and mounds of mud to channel the water in one direction while he dug for treasure in another.

And the water from the lovely river was spilling everywhere, all along the bank and round the trees and in dirty, long channels and over the grass in muddy little bursts and right around Dan in his mud island in the middle of it all. And Dan had a shovel in his hand, the one from the garden at home, and he was digging very hard with it, and he was quite unconcerned for what he was doing.

Kerry rushed across the waterways where once the bank of the lovely river had been and into the river and he floundered up to his waist in water and to the place where Dan was digging, and he picked up Dan with one strong arm and his shovel with the other, and he threw Dan one way, onto the bank, and the shovel the other, into the deepest part of the river where it flowed fastest of all. Then he floundered back to land after his brother and set about him, beating him and shaking him and all the time there was a dreadful, black noise inside his head, and it was the westels crying out from deep in the waters.

So Kerry drove his brother away. And after the shouting and the fury and the anger had taken place and finally gone, he looked at the spoiling and thought that this must be the height of all sadness in life. But another thing happened, and it made all Kerry's sadness seem nothing, so sad did he become and so black inside himself and so despairing and lost, and lonely too.

For the westels appeared on the surface of the water, one after another. They were on their backs, lying quite still and as in death, paler than even before, carried by the strongest current right away from him. Mud and river scum clung to them, running over their lovely, sad faces and their pale, almost transparent bodies, and like a great dead army they were taken downstream and away upon the brown, thick water. And as they went, their crying grew less and when they had gone, their crying was gone.

Then it was very quiet indeed and Kerry felt alone, more than ever before in his life. For the westels had departed from their lovely place and he had lost his new and his dearest of all friends and he had destroyed them by being their friend and he had destroyed a good place in the land as well.

Kerry lay on the ground in one of the channels that Dan had made, and he wept. He wept for the spoiling of the lovely river, and he wept for the spoiling of the creatures that had been his friends. He wept for the loss of his treasures that they had given to him. He wept for his mother and Dan and because he couldn't go home and didn't want to go home any more. And for greed and for the ugliness in the land he wept too. He longed that the land might be good and there might be real gladness, and for the time when it wouldn't be possible for people to scatter and spoil. He wept as the westels had taught him to weep, but the westels had gone and he wept alone.

After a long time, the fleetings came to him. They came all around him and they touched him with their wings, for comfort, and he was comforted by their touch.

'What will you do?' said the fleetings.

Kerry remembered something that the westels had said to him before they had gone.

'Build a house,' he said to the fleetings. 'Find work to do. Live by the river.' Then he remembered how the westels had said he should find a wife and that they would be friends to his children and his children's children for all time, and he began to cry again, because the westels had gone, and this would never take place.

'The river will be good again,' said the fleetings. 'And the westels will come back. They aren't dead, for we creatures can't die, as you people do. When the river is good, they'll come back, they'll remember how you were their friend, for they wouldn't give friendship lightly and they loved you. When the spoiling is passed, you will be friends again.'

So Kerry remained. He built a little house by the river and he found work to do in the land. And in good time he was wed and had children, just as the westels had told him to do, and he called the children Bright Stone and Gold Sand, in memory of the treasures that had been stolen from him. And despite all the good things he had, and the love of his wife and his children, he was the saddest man in all the land.

But as the years passed and with the care that Kerry and his good wife and his children gave to it, the river was repaired from the damage that had been done. And when the years had passed, the westels did return, just as the fleetings had said. And then Kerry was the happiest man in all the land.

And Kerry's children, and his children's children, lived in

the little house that he made by the river, and the westels were their friends, as they had promised to Kerry, from that time to this, and they loved Kerry's family as people had not been loved by creatures ever before.

Five

CONCERNING THE CREATURES AND THE WICKED ENEMY OF THE KING

King Gerald had a wicked enemy in the land where the people lived. And the wicked enemy saw the friendship between the people and the good creatures and how with the help of the creatures, people had learned to love the land and to care for it. And because the land was King Gerald's, the wicked enemy sought to destroy it beyond all repair. This is the story of the wicked enemy and the creatures and how the wicked enemy sought to spoil the creatures, as the people had been spoiled.

It was autumn. It hardly seemed that the leaves had time to dislodge themselves from the trees, and then, in the night, the frost came down. It covered everything. In the valley, people rushed around making winter preparations and up on the southern hill, the creatures rushed around too. The fleetings took themselves off to other places, and the cotties hurried about, shivering and huddled together, trying to collect things in for the long, cold season that had come so suddenly upon them all.

They were out in the pastures on the top of the southern hill. They were all very busy and they were all very cold and they were all very cheerful too, as cotties usually are, and the sun was shining and the air was clear and it was a fine day to be the first of winter.

A fleeting came out of the dark hill across the other side of the wild wood, and high into the sky. It rose like a giant moon, white and magnificent, and it rose slowly.

The cotties took no notice of it, because they saw fleetings in the sky all the time. But then the fleeting unfurled its white wings. It spread itself out right across the blue sky and it was larger and more magnificent and more beautiful, too, than any fleeting that the cotties had ever seen. They stopped their work on the southern hill and they stared at the fleeting and they wondered what it was doing over the dark hill when all the other fleetings had decided to go away, and they wondered where it had come from and who it was.

A coldness crept up them all from the ground, and they became very quiet among themselves. There was something very strange about the fleeting. They could not turn away from it or go to some other place where they could not see it or even get on with their work. They could only stare at it.

Time passed, and the creature hung in the sky, and it did not move and it had nothing to say. Then, at mid-morning, when the sun had started melting the frost, it folded its wings in around itself and began its descent, slowly, and silent as it had come, into the dark hill.

The cotties watched its going and they stood quite still, and when it had gone they stood quite still for a very long time. Then they stirred themselves, for the winter was coming and there were many things to do, and they carried on with the work they had been doing before. They just picked up their things and worked as before and they said nothing about what they had seen and nothing about what they had felt. And when the work was done and the day was done too, they left the pastures of the southern hill and went their different ways.

Next morning, the frost was all over the grass again with its lovely patterns, and lying upon the spiders' webs in the hedges and the backs of the leaves and showing the little hairs sticking up like prickles on them. And the sun was shining again, and the sky was blue and it was crisp and cold and a fine second day for winter.

The cotties came out into the pastures. They had new jobs to do and they got on with their jobs, getting ready for winter, and they worked quickly and quietly and not very cheerfully and most unlike how cotties would usually work.

They had not been out long when the fleeting came out of the dark hill across the other side of the wild wood, and rose high in the sky. It was as before, a magnificent creature and a great creature, too, spreading itself out in the sky. The cotties put aside their work and they stood and stared at the fleeting and they said nothing at all. So they remained for a long time, and at mid-morning, once again, the fleeting folded its wings in about itself and descended towards the southern hill.

It disappeared into the hill and its disappearance was release for the cotties. They shook themselves and picked up their things and, once again, they tried to get on with their jobs. But this time, there could be no getting on with jobs, for the cotties were full of strange feelings and deeply stirred, and they left the pastures, one after another, and went back to their own places, and they were sombre and silent and they stayed in their little places all day long, thinking about the strange fleeting and trying to understand the feeling that had come into them. And this was very unlike the exuberant cotties, and very mysterious.

Next morning, they came back to the pastures. They did not work. They sat in the pastures and waited for the fleeting to appear. There was no birdsong and no wind and no sound in the land at all. And soon the fleeting did appear and it rose up in the clear sky.

It was crying. It cried as it rose and it cried as it hung in the sky with its wings opened out. There was no sound at all, except for its cry. The cotties sat still and they looked at the fleeting and they listened to its crying, and the sight of the fleeting filled their eyes and its sound filled their ears and rang in their heads. They sat till it had gone, and when it had gone, it left silence behind, and after a time the cotties stirred themselves and started to move.

They did not speak to each other. They did not attempt to do work in the pastures. They left all their things and they walked down the pastures and through the fields where the wheat would grow and through the orchards at the bottom of the hill, and they were not the quick, excitable creatures that cotties usually were, and they did not move as cotties usually moved at all. They moved like dreamers, or people without feelings, and in this strange way they came into the valley. They walked in the valley for some long time, and as they walked they seemed to recover themselves very slowly and to wake from their dreams, and gradually they were like cotties again and not dreamers.

When they were like cotties again and themselves again, they did all the usual cottie things like rushing about among themselves in a panic and shouting and gesturing and surging like waves on a shore and not knowing what should be done. Gradually they calmed themselves down and they shared with each other the way that they felt, and it seemed to them that they had made an escape from the southern hill and that something was wrong up there, but they didn't know why and they didn't know how, and they wondered about the strange fleeting and why it had cried its sad cry and where it had come from.

They decided that they needed some help and they said that they'd go to King Gerald's Oak. King Gerald's Oak was the centre of the king's land, and it was a perfect tree and quite unspoiled, and there were cotties who lived in the Oak and these cotties were its keepers and they were the leaders of all the cotties in the land.

So they followed the valley along to the Oak, and they came to the Oak and they called for the keepers to come down and help them. The keepers of King Gerald's Oak got out of the tree and came before them, and the cotties became very excited again and very heated and they all tried to tell everything at once, so that it was a long time before the keepers could extract a whole, accurate and understandable tale out of them.

And when they had the whole story, it all seemed very slight to the keepers. They saw fleetings every day. Some were larger than others! Some were more beautiful! They admitted they never had seen a fleeting who cried, but why had the cotties not asked why the fleeting was crying? As far as the keepers could see, the whole matter was vastly enlarged upon.

But the cotties insisted that the keepers had not seen the fleeting as they'd seen it or felt what they'd felt. And if they had seen it and known how it made them feel, then they would understand and know something was wrong.

So the keepers agreed to come with the cotties to the southern hill in order to see what the cotties had seen and to feel what they felt. They packed up a few things and they went with the cotties. On the way, they issued the cotties with mild reproaches for letting their excitable natures and imaginations overcome them. In the valley, the cotties were half-inclined to agree, but when they got to the slopes of the southern hill, they became quiet, and they no longer agreed that they'd let their cottie natures get the better of them. For the strange feeling was upon them again.

So they came to the high pastures and it was early morning again. And they stood about in the high pastures on the cold, frosty grass, and they all waited together.

Soon, the magnificent fleeting rose out of the dark hill. And as soon as it rose, the keepers of King Gerald's Oak knew the strange feeling that had come upon the other cotties, and they were silent and still, as all the cotties were silent and still.

So the fleeting rose, and it hung in the sky, and at mid-morning it descended again. And with its rising and its unfurling in the sky above the dark hill and its hanging there and falling again and disappearing into the hill, came these words, and they replaced the sad cry it had made before, and they were loud in the stillness, and they rang in the cotties' heads and could not be forgotten.

'King Gerald has abandoned us,' said the fleeting, 'King Gerald has abandoned us,' and it repeated these words over and over again, all the time that it was in the sky and until it had gone.

When it had gone, they remained on the southern hill, and they were no longer excited, noisy creatures as cotties usually are, but they were cold again and still again and grim. After some time, the keepers of King Gerald's Oak stirred themselves and they addressed the other cotties in quiet, solemn voices, for they had seen for themselves what the cotties had seen and knew what they knew.

'This is not right,' they said. 'Something here is not right. No good creature in King Gerald's land would say words like these words, about the king.'

The cotties agreed that things were not right. For they all were afraid, and no good thing in the land would make fear, and they could not believe, not any of them, that King

Gerald had abandoned them. But the fleetings were good creatures, and there was no wickedness in them and there could be no untruth in any of the creatures, and they could not understand how a fleeting could say an untrue thing, and they were all very disturbed by these things and confused.

'We must look for the other fleetings,' said the keepers of King Gerald's Oak. 'We must see what they say, and find out if all fleetings are saying these strange things. We must find out about this creature too, and see if the others know where it comes from and if they know anything about what is happening here.'

And the keepers divided the cotties into little bands, and the little bands prepared themselves for their journeys and they went off, down the southern hill and right across the land, to see where the fleetings might be.

As they went, the words 'King Gerald has abandoned us' and the sad crying of the strange fleeting rang inside their heads. They wondered, all of them, if some dreadful thing might have happened and the king had abandoned them after all. Then they were ashamed for wondering such a wicked thing, and tried to put the thought away from them. But the words would not leave them.

So little bands of cotties went right across King Gerald's land. They passed through the valleys and the hill country and along by the rivers where the westels lived and the great lakes too. And the westels would not speak to them, but sometimes very distantly they heard the westels crying a terrible cry, and they thought that perhaps the westels had heard what they heard, for the westels could hear many things in the land, and that they were afraid as they all were afraid.

They were gone a long time. Winter was firmly established when they found where the fleetings had gone. They were tired with the searching, and they were afraid and cold and grim, for the words of the strange fleeting were still in their heads, and they carried them like a most terrible burden.

The fleetings were beside the seashore. They greeted the cotties with surprise and pleasure, but then they saw that something was wrong and the cotties told them their news, and the fleetings were filled with dismay. For they had not heard this strange thing, and they said it was not possible that King Gerald had abandoned them, for King Gerald was a good king and he was true, and they said even now there were fleetings with him in his palace far away. They said they would come right away to this fleeting who said these strange words, and they were confused, as the cotties were confused, that a good creature in the land and one of their own kind could say an untrue word.

So the fleetings took the cotties up into their wings. They went back along the land and, as they journeyed, they gathered up all the grim little bands of cotties that the keepers had sent out, and they took them all back, as fast as they could, to the southern hill. As they came nearer to the southern hill, they became quieter and quieter because the strange fleeting was there, and because they were afraid of it.

It was night by the time they arrived, a wet, winter night and quite dark. It was dark as they flew up the southern hill, but as they came out from among the trees to the pastures on the top of it, they found the sky by the dark hill had become very bright. And when they came to rest in the pastures, they saw that the fleeting was there, hanging over the dark hill above them all, white and very beautiful, more beautiful than the cotties had remembered, and seeming to shine in the dark.

'King Gerald will not come to us. King Gerald will not come,' it was saying. 'King Gerald will not come to us. King Gerald will not come.' And it said these words over and over again, and its voice was full of sorrow, and it was a strong, lovely voice and they could not help but listen to the beautiful voice and the terrible words.

So they stood on the pastures of the southern hill. They knew that the words were a wickedness, but the voice drew them to it and the words seemed to drown them, and they were drawn and repelled at the same time. The words never ceased. They all listened, the cotties and their leaders who were the keepers of King Gerald's Oak, and the fleetings, and the westels heard too, for they were crying, distantly from their deep places.

The keepers of the Oak shook themselves. They did not want to listen to these dreadful words and they did not want to enjoy a voice that said terrible things. They started to shout out to the fleeting that hung over the dark hill and they wanted to know why the king would not come to them and how the strange fleeting knew such a thing.

Their shouting seemed to awake the other creatures on the southern hill. The fleetings jumped up and would not let the keepers ask their questions, nor would they let them speak with the fleeting in the sky. And the cotties began to rush about in a panic and to seek some escape from the voice and the words.

'This is no fleeting,' said the fleetings. 'You must not speak to it. This creature is wicked. It is not one of us. There is only one thing it can be. We must go to the tines!'

And as the fleetings said this thing, that the creature was not one of them, the other creatures knew, quite surely, that there was only one thing it could be. There was only one creature who spoke wickedness and untruth. The sight in the sky could only be the one who disguised itself in many forms and could deceive with disguises, the wicked enemy of King Gerald. And they were angry with themselves for not knowing this long ago and preparing to fight with the enemy. For the battle was all upon them and they were unprepared. They knew they should not listen to the words of the enemy, but they were repeated over and over again and the voice was so beautiful that they could not help but listen to it.

The fleetings cried out once again that they should go to the tines, and the cotties climbed into the wings of the fleetings and they went quickly away from the southern hill and up to the high hills and the caves to the tines who with their secrets and wisdom might know what to do.

But the enemy would not leave them. As they went to the high hills, it followed them, and it chanted its words, 'King Gerald will not come to us. King Gerald will not come,' and these words filled all their heads and were a very great pain to them and none could escape from the words. Down on the land too, the westels cried mournfully and the pain was theirs too, and they all cried, and in this way they came to the high hills and the caves where the tines might be found.

They went into the caves and the tines came to them and when they were there all together, the enemy hung outside the entrance of the caves and it repeated its words and the tines heard them too and cried as the others had cried, and they all were distressed. The cotties rushed about in the caves of the tines, from the dark places to the mouth of the caves and back to the dark places again, and they had all the caves in disorder and chaos. The fleetings folded their wings in on themselves and tried to bury themselves away from the words of the enemy and found they could not. And the westels cried in the distant places and the tines tried to understand all that had happened and set their wise old minds in order so that a plan could be made.

Then the tines went away and the creatures thought that they were deserted and cried all the more. And when they cried all the more, the wicked enemy chanted louder and thought it had become triumphant over the creatures, and it chanted its terrible words faster too, and the more the creatures cried, the more it thought they were defeated and the more excited it became and the louder and faster it chanted. But in all of this chaos, the tines returned, very great in number and all pale and all grim as the other creatures were grim. But they were crying no more and they were a quietness within all the chaos.

They brought out trumpets and cymbals, wrapped all about in fine cloth and they made the creatures be quiet and then they addressed them all. And although they spoke quietly and the enemy was loud, all the creatures could hear very clearly the words that the tines had to say and were strengthened and encouraged by them. And the tines remained quiet and controlled all the time that they spoke, but they were struggling all of this time not to listen to the wicked enemy and struggling, too, in order to stay calm.

'We shall defeat the enemy,' they said. 'We shall drive the enemy away. We tines know secret ways of weakening its powers. But because we have listened to the words of the enemy, we shall suffer from this attack. Until the day when

King Gerald comes, we shall remember these words and they will give us no peace.

'We have thought people spoilers in the land,' said the tines. 'And so they are. But we have not reckoned with the power of the great spoiler before. We have been unprepared and we have been attacked. This is a dark day for us all!'

Then the creatures began to cry again and the tines said, 'We have no power to finish the enemy for ever. We can defeat it for now, but not for all time. So we must hide from this enemy who could hurt us again.'

And the creatures knew that they would have to disperse into dark and distant places in the land and they stopped all their crying and became very quiet, thinking about this, and very solemn as well.

Then the tines gave the cymbals and the trumpets to the creatures and they said that the creatures must bang on the cymbals and blow on the trumpets and they must dance and they must sing too and they must make a very great din because they were going to march upon the wicked enemy with the tines at their head and it was important that they did not listen to the words that the enemy said. And the tines said they had secret words that they would pronounce before the wicked enemy and with these words they would drive it away.

So the creatures lined themselves up behind the great tines. Out in the sky above the caves, the wicked enemy hung low and it chanted fast and loud all its words concerning the king. And as they marched out, the creatures thought they could not help but listen to these dreadful words and be harmed by them, and they did not sing and they did not dance and they did not blow the trumpets or bang on the cymbals.

'Sing!' cried the tines. 'Shout! Make a great noise! How can we do what has to be done if we hear what the enemy is saying?'

And deep from the distant places, a singing began. And loud all around them, the song of the westels came through, the victory song. Then the creatures took the trumpets and cymbals and they played on the trumpets and cymbals and they sang very loud and the westels sang loud, and the old tines marched on and the creatures came dancing behind and they danced very hard, and whenever the words of the wicked enemy came through to them, they sang all the louder and played all the louder and danced harder too.

So the straight old tines marched upon the wicked enemy of King Gerald, and the creatures who loved the king danced behind. And the straight old tines pronounced secret words as they marched on the enemy, words of wisdom from the dark places where they lived, and all the creatures sang out the name of the king. And in this manner, they progressed down from the high hills, driving the enemy before them in the sky, and along to the southern hill.

The wicked enemy cried out louder and faster, and it hung over the dark hill and all the creatures cried out the king's name many times, and the tines said their secret things and they all made their music, and they were very strong and the enemy was weak, and in this way was the enemy driven and defeated. For it hung in its whiteness and beauty above the dark hill and the dawn was creeping slowly around them all and the light was coming that would drive the tines back into their dark places. And suddenly, the enemy collapsed like a ball of smoke into the dark hill and was gone. And the land where it fell became quite barren as though nothing had grown on it ever.

The dawn opened out on them all. It was morning. It was very quiet. The enemy and the words of the enemy were gone. The creatures stopped singing and shouting and playing their instruments. The southern hill was no longer a strange and a frightening place as it had become for them all. They stood in the pastures and observed all these things and then they began to shout and to leap about and the fleetings flew up into the sky and made beautiful chains right across the sky and the cotties just surged about and the song of the westels had gone to a very soft sound, and the tines just stood, tired and weak and strained because the daylight was growing in the land, and they looked out at the bare place where the enemy had fallen.

Then the tines called all the creatures around. 'We have defeated the enemy,' they said. 'We have driven the enemy into the dark hill. But we have no power to defeat the enemy for always and we must all prepare places to hide from the future attacks. For we all know the enemy's power now!'

And the creatures became quiet. The fleetings came down from the sky and the cotties stopped surging. For they had seen the real spoiler at work in the land, and they knew the power it had, and they knew they must hide and must prepare themselves for other attacks. And when they were quiet, in the dawn on the southern hill, the words of the enemy echoed distantly inside their heads, 'King Gerald will not come to us. King Gerald will not come,' and they knew that the words would always be with them, distantly inside their heads, until the king came.

So the battle was won, but the creatures were sad. They separated and they found secret, distant, more hidden places in which they could stay. Sometimes the words, 'King Gerald will not come,' came into their heads and whenever they did, they remembered this time when they had driven the enemy into the dark hill with trumpets and cymbals and dancing and singing and shouting the name of the king and with the secret words of the tines who lived under the earth and were wise. And in their secret, hidden places, they awaited the time when King Gerald would come.

Six

BASKETWEAVER AND THE BOY WITH NO EYES

This is the story of Basketweaver and Old Woman. And it is the story of their son, Youngest Son, and the stranger who came to their home and who lived with them all, the boy with no eyes.

There was a quiet river bank, a long way from the other people who lived in King Gerald's land. It was just a simple place where the river turned slowly and where Basketweaver and Old Woman lived in a little house with four windows staring out on to the river and four rooms that were very dark when you went into them, and very small too. And it was the place where they lived all their lives.

And it was the place where the westels lived too. For Basketweaver was the special friend of the westels, as his father before him had been, and his father before him too. And when they were young, he and Old Woman went down to the westels and about in the land to the other creatures too, and great celebrations were had by them all. But the westels had changed and the other creatures had changed. For a sadness had come to them all and they became distant and shy and Basketweaver and Old Woman spent night-times and holidays walking about in the land and down by the river, remembering things and wondering about the sadness that had come to the creatures, and blaming the times, for the times were so bad, for driving the creatures away.

Now Basketweaver wove baskets to sell in the market. He sat every day by the river, soaking his canes and bending them into the shapes that he wanted and making them into his baskets. Old Woman bore sons to Basketweaver, and while he worked by the river, she brought up the sons and taught them good things and when they were ready and old enough, she sent them away to find work for themselves in the land, or to find adventures or perhaps to find wives. Only her son, Youngest Son, was at home, and soon he would go.

One day, Old Woman was alone in the house and she was sitting in the light of the window making lace for the market. She was a quick, little woman with bright, beady eyes and a tiny head covered with grey hair, and sometimes she looked like a child, and sometimes she looked like a very old person.

Youngest Son opened the door and looked round it and saw her sitting in the light of the window, and she looked up and saw him and he said good-day and smiled nervously, and he stood with his head round the door and hesitated about coming in, and seemed very awkward.

Old Woman put down her lace and looked hard at her son with her sharp little eyes, and she said, 'Well, you'd better come in,' very briskly, as though she cared not at all to be seeing him.

But despite her brisk voice, she was glad he was home. For Youngest Son had gone off on adventures, and of all of her sons, he was the least able to care for himself. And she noticed his shuffling about and his awkwardness, and she told him to sit down where she could look at him properly, and to say what was wrong.

Youngest Son didn't sit down. He came into the room and shut the door firmly behind him. When it was shut, he leaned up against it and squared up his shoulders and Old Woman thought how silly he looked, and when he spoke, she thought how silly he sounded, as well.

'Mother,' said Youngest Son, 'there's a person outside right now, and that person is the ugliest person in the whole land, and you never saw such a horrible looking person in the whole of your life. That person is my friend, and I want him to stay with us.'

'Come and sit down,' said Old Woman. 'Tell me about your horrible friend.' And she picked up her lace again and bent her head over it and smiled to herself because nothing was wrong after all. Just a friend with a horrible face, and she'd seen plenty of those in her life.

Youngest Son sat by his mother and did as she told him. He told his adventures. All three days of them. He told of how he had met his new friend, and how his friend had come from very distant places and had warned him not to go to those places because of the terrible illness raging in them. It seemed that many people had died, and many more people had been dreadfully disfigured and struck in most terrible ways.

Old Woman had heard of such illnesses. She picked at her lace and listened very quietly until Youngest Son had finished telling his adventures, and then she put down the lace again and said, 'Well then, let's go and meet your new friend.'

Youngest Son jumped up and became very agitated and surged all around her, seeming to go in every direction at once, and issuing all sorts of warnings about what his friend looked like and how she must prepare herself, and saying too that his friend had lost all his family in the illness, and it was only right that he should have somewhere to stay.

Old Woman just swept him aside. She opened the door and went out into the porch to meet Youngest Son's friend, and he was sitting out there, waiting to know if he could stay.

The friend was surprisingly young. He was a boy, hardly as old as Youngest Son even. He was smaller than Old Woman and he had tiny hands and feet and a little, thin body. He had very smooth features, and soft, pale skin, and he was very delicate too, and had pale yellow hair. He had one disfiguring mark. For it was as though the boy's eyes had been winkled out of their sockets like fish out of shells. The boy had no eyes.

Old Woman looked at the boy with no eyes. She took the boy's hand by way of a greeting and asked him inside, and she gave him some food, and when he had eaten, she asked him about himself.

Youngest Son fussed all around her and worried that the sight of the boy's eyeless face might have upset her, and he made her quite cross, for she had seen many worse things than a head with no eyes in it in her long, old life. So she

sent Youngest Son down to the river to fetch Basketweaver, and when he had gone, it was very quiet and she could pay proper attention to what the boy said of himself.

The boy's story was much as Youngest Son had told it, and it was a very sad story too. Old Woman was sorry for the boy because he had no family left. But she felt uncomfortable sitting with him, for sometimes, as he talked, she felt sure he could see her, even though he had no eyes, and this feeling distracted her quite considerably because it was such a silly and unreasonable feeling to have.

Basketweaver came into the house and he spoke with the boy too. Then he sent the boy out with Youngest Son to do some little jobs, and he and Old Woman talked together. They both had the same feeling, as though the boy really could see them, and they both felt uncomfortable with him. But because he was young, and because Youngest Son seemed so fond of him, and because he had lost his family and had nowhere to go, they said it was good that he should stay with them.

So the boy stayed. Youngest Son was all contentment because the boy was good company for him. And he was good company for them all. He was a quiet boy and fitted in readily with family activities and he entertained them with the stories of where he had been and what he had done, and the amazing things that had happened all over the land during his travels.

During the day, when Basketweaver was down by the river and Old Woman worked in the house, the boy would go from one to the other, looking for jobs, and when he was given them to do, he would work thoroughly and to the best of his ability as well. And he worked very quickly, and his hands were very clever and light, and he did many helpful things for them.

And at night and on holidays, when Basketweaver and Old Woman took Youngest Son about in the land and down to the river and showed him the places where westels might be found, and told him their stories concerning the creatures and taught him the things that they knew about King Gerald's land, the boy would go with them. And where Youngest Son was bored and thought their little stories silly, the boy was all interest, and where Youngest Son was silent and sullen, the boy was full of questions, and they told the boy many things that they knew concerning the land, and the good creatures that lived in it, and the king of the land.

So, in every respect, it seemed that the boy with no eyes was as perfect a guest as could be desired. But Basketweaver and Old Woman were still uncomfortable in the boy's company, and they could not bring themselves to like him. And the boy knew this.

One day, Youngest Son and the boy with no eyes went out onto the river in Basketweaver's little boat. Youngest Son wanted to get out of jobs for a day, and they decided to go on a journey and see how far the river would take them. They set out early, and sometimes they rowed, and sometimes they let the current of the river carry them. They were in no hurry. They were going nowhere in particular. And it was a lovely day for being lazy and having a good, quiet time.

They were eating and drinking and drifting with the current, and the boy with no eyes suddenly said, 'When did your brothers leave home?'

Youngest Son told him.

'Why did they leave?' said the boy.

Youngest Son told him that too. They were all expected to leave. They were brought up to leave. They were to go out in the land and look for adventures and find work to be done and find themselves wives and have their own children. All the brothers had gone when Old Woman had said they were ready.

'Well now,' said the boy, and he smiled very gently to himself. 'And who told you that?'

Youngest Son looked up at the boy, and just for a moment he had the thought that the boy really could see him, and it seemed that they looked at each other for a second or so. Then the boy changed the subject very quickly, and he asked Youngest Son to describe to him the place where they were, and he asked Youngest Son to set up the fishing-line, so that he could fish.

But a new feeling had come into Youngest Son. He would not describe the place where they were, nor would he set up the fishing-line. And this little lumpy feeling inside of him wanted to know why the boy smiled such a secret little smile, and why he had asked all those questions. The new little feeling wanted to know very much more.

But the boy would not tell him, and eventually Youngest Son set up the line and he drank a lot more, and then, when the new little feeling seemed to have gone, he started rowing again, but slowly and thoughtfully.

Another day, Youngest Son was chopping up wood, and the boy with no eyes was feeling his way along the ground, collecting the bits as they flew from the axe.

Youngest Son suddenly put down his axe and called to the boy, and he sat on the ground and the boy sat beside him, and Youngest Son said, 'I want to know why you were asking those things on the river. About my brothers, I mean.'

The boy looked awkward, with his mouth all pursed up and a frown across his forehead. He said nothing at all, but the little lumpy feeling that had come to Youngest Son on the river was upon him again, and he got very cross that the boy would not speak, and became very insistent, and it all seemed much more important than he had thought it before, because the boy would not speak of it.

At last, the boy with no eyes became cross, and Youngest Son was quite surprised, for he never had seen the boy cross about anything.

'Look,' said the boy with no eyes, 'if I said that Old Woman was a liar and told you your brothers didn't leave when she told them to, but ran away from this place, what would you think of that?'

And he got up from his place beside Youngest Son and went right away, feeling his way along from tree to tree and by the side of the fence.

Youngest Son came right after him, and he grabbed him very hard, and would not let him go.

'What do you mean?' he said, 'What are you talking about?' Then he began to shout. 'Go on,' he shouted, 'say it again!'

The boy seemed very calm, all the time that Youngest Son held him and shouted. And when Youngest Son finished his shouting, he spoke very quietly, and he sounded very sure of what he said. And as he spoke, it was almost as though he was very much older than he looked, because he was so sure of himself.

'I have lived in other places, and you have not,' he said. 'I know more about life in the land than you do. And I tell you, the way that you live is not the way that all people live. Not all people are like Basketweaver and Old Woman. Not all people keep their sons prisoners!'

The little lumpy feeling was a very big feeling in Youngest Son now. At first, he wanted to hit at the boy with no eyes for saying that he was a prisoner, and he wanted to make him stop saying any more. But the quietness with which the boy spoke made him quiet too, and he found that he wanted to hear all the boy said, and he just listened.

'If Old Woman really sent her sons away,' said the boy with no eyes, 'why hasn't she sent you? You're old enough to live on your own in the land. Do you want to know what I think about your brothers? I think they escaped. I think they couldn't live any more with the lessons about good and bad and the king of the land whom they never could see and the creatures they never could see but were supposed to believe were there. I think they didn't want to be poor when they could go away and become rich, and they didn't want to live in a tiny house when they could live in a big house. I think they wanted to make fortunes and have real adventures and be very rich, and they escaped, and that's why.'

Youngest Son was stirred by these things, and the feeling inside him seemed very strong. But somehow, he wished that he had not listened to them and he was angry with himself and he took his anger out on the boy and shouted at him and said if he thought such things, perhaps he'd like to find some other place where he could live.

But then the boy stopped seeming so much older than his age and so sure of himself. He screwed up his face and became very red all over and started to make funny noises in his throat and to shake, and Youngest Son realized that if the boy had eyes, they would be wet and he would be crying.

The boy said that he hadn't wanted to say any of these things and that Youngest Son had made him. He said that he didn't want to think such things, it wasn't his fault if he thought them, and he said that he would go right away because he had lost Youngest Son's friendship, the only friendship he had. Youngest Son felt ashamed of himself for treating a poor boy with no family and no eyes in this way, and he started to cry.

So they became friends again. The boy with no eyes promised never to mention these matters again. And they returned to the wood block and got on with their work, Youngest Son chopping and the boy with no eyes crawling along the ground collecting the wood. So the matter was dropped. And Basketweaver and Old Woman knew nothing of what had taken place.

One day, Old Woman was at the back of the house planting vegetables. Her tiny old back was aching and she sat on the earth and rested very quietly. And as she sat resting and looking about her, she saw a cottie come out from between the trees at the far end of the vegetables.

Now, when Old Woman saw the cottie at the edge of her garden, she sat very still and hardly breathed and she hoped that the creature would come and speak to her and not just pass on. For she never saw creatures to speak to any more, but only distantly. And it seemed that the cottie was coming to her, for it came right out from the trees and looked straight at her and she smiled at the little cottie, and the little cottie smiled at her, and it came very close.

Then, quite unexpectedly, it stopped smiling, and it turned round very quickly and it went right away between the trees, and it left Old Woman feeling frightened and not knowing why.

'I say,' called a voice, and Old Woman turned round sharply. The boy with no eyes had come to the side of the house. 'Do you need any help getting up?'

'No,' said Old Woman. 'No thank you. I can manage,' and she told the boy to go away and leave her alone, and she spoke very sharply.

The boy went away, and Old Woman sat on the earth with her heart beating about inside of her. She was quite sure that the boy with no eyes had driven the cottie away, and she was afraid of the boy with no eyes. She pulled herself up from the ground and took all her tools back to the house, and she tottered very slowly back into the house, a little old scrap of a woman, and when she got in, she found Youngest Son there, sitting in front of the fire, when he should be out by the river with Basketweaver.

Youngest Son could not forget the words of the boy with no eyes. They just kept on repeating themselves inside his head, and he sat by the fire, feeling sorry for himself and thinking that he really was a prisoner, with Old Woman and Basketweaver looking after him.

'What are you doing?' said Old Woman. 'Shouldn't you be helping your father?'

'I'm thinking about leaving,' said Youngest Son. 'It's time that I went. I'm as old as my brothers were when they went away.'

Old Woman was too shaken by the boy with no eyes and the cottie to take very much notice, and she dismissed Youngest Son very lightly by shaking her tiny head and saying, 'That would be silly, Youngest Son. You don't yet know how to take care of yourself properly. Your brothers were much more able to manage than you would be.' Then she went right away and got on with new jobs and forgot about Youngest Son.

Now this was very true, and if Youngest Son had thought more about it, he would have had to agree with Old Woman, but he was cross because she dismissed him so easily and considered his wanting to leave as a matter of silliness. And he felt that the boy with no eyes was quite right, and he was a prisoner, and he never would get away.

There was another thing that he remembered too. It was a long time before he mentioned it, but one day, full of curiosity, he said to the boy with no eyes,

'Tell me about being rich.'

The boy was upset. He said that he couldn't possibly talk of such things. He had made a promise not to mention them again, and he was going to keep his promise too. Youngest Son tried very hard to insist, and in the end the boy ran away from him and went down to Basketweaver beside the river and asked if there were jobs he could do, and the subject was closed for the time.

Basketweaver gave some little job to the boy, and he got on with his own work. Sometimes, he looked up and he watched the boy with the job that he'd given him. He watched his swift, deft little hands and the way that he worked, and he looked at the boy's face, and what he saw puzzled him. For it seemed that the boy was thinking very deeply about some matter, with creases across his forehead, and his mouth all pulled in, and the thinking was hardly in line with the job he was doing. Basketweaver had noticed a thoughtfulness about the boy many times, and he would have given much to know what the boy thought about, for in all the time that he was with them, Basketweaver liked the boy with no eyes less and less.

Now, while they were down by the river, both of them working, a very strange thing happened. Basketweaver had been looking at the boy and thinking these things concerning him, and he took his eyes off the boy and looked into the deep water out in the middle of the river. For a moment, he thought that he heard a westel, and he was very excited and hoped that the westel would show itself, for he longed to talk to westels and have good times with them again. Then he thought that he had not heard it, and that he was just full of foolish imagination, and while he thought this thing, the westel appeared. It came up in the water until it was just beneath the surface, and he could see its light, childlike face. But the westel turned quickly in the water, and instead of coming out of it as it had seemed it would do, it went back into the dark places and disappeared.

Basketweaver thought instantly that the westel must have seen the boy. For westels were shy creatures and not generally taken to appearing before people. Basketweaver turned towards the boy. And he wished that he had not turned towards him, for the way that the boy looked made him feel colder inside himself than he would have thought it possible to be.

For it was as though the boy with no eyes had seen the westel and had driven it away. He had stopped working, and he was leaning forward with his face over the water, and the places where his eyes should have been seemed to be scanning the water. And a most horrible expression was on his face too, and his mouth seemed to be all twisted up, and Basketweaver, who had never been afraid in the whole of his life, was afraid.

At night, when they were all in bed, Basketweaver wanted to tell this to Old Woman. But each time he began to whisper to her, he had the most uncomfortable feeling, as though the boy with no eyes, asleep in the next room, could see what he was doing and was listening to what he said. In fact, he felt this so strongly that he even got out of bed and he went to the door and lifted the latch ever so quietly and looked into the room where the boys slept. The boy with no eyes was asleep in his bed, and Basketweaver felt very foolish and went back to bed, and Old Woman whispered not to worry, he could tell her tomorrow, and they both tried to sleep.

Next day was market day. Old Woman did a thing she had never done before. She said that Basketweaver and she were too busy for market, and Youngest Son and the boy with no eyes should go alone for once, to sell the baskets and lace for them. She made them some food and gave them some ale for the journey and told them to go early and quick, or else the market would be over by the time they arrived.

When they had gone, she sat Basketweaver down and made him tell her about the westel and the way the boy had looked at the river. And she told him her own story, concerning the cottie, and how she had thought that the boy had driven the cottie away.

While Basketweaver and Old Woman exchanged fears and suspicions concerning the boy with no eyes, Youngest Son and the boy sold the baskets and lace. They counted up their money and set out for home again when they were sure that they had the correct amount.

'Tell me about being rich,' said Youngest Son.

The boy with no eyes took the money that they had just made on the sale of the baskets and lace, and he turned it over in his hands, and he made no protests about not wanting to say anything or to speak out against Basketweaver and Old Woman, and he made no more mention of the promises he had made.

He just said, 'I'll tell you one thing. This isn't being rich!' And he threw the money up into the air and it fell all over the road.

Youngest Son rushed about picking it up again, and the boy started talking and it seemed from the way that he talked that he was not young after all and that he was not even a boy, but that he was old and knowledgeable and a very powerful person who knew just about everything.

He told Youngest Son what being rich was like, and he said that if Youngest Son lived as Basketweaver and Old Woman lived, he would never be rich. He listed ways of becoming rich and he said what things Youngest Son would be able to do if he was rich.

He even said that Youngest Son could help Basketweaver and Old Woman because they were so poor and they needed help. And he laughed at this idea, and then Youngest Son laughed too, and the new, lumpy feeling that first came to him down on the river was all over him and he was excited and red in the face with excitement, and he laughed very hard, and the more that he laughed, the more that the boy with no eyes laughed as well.

Then Youngest Son said that he wanted to be on his own. For now that he knew about being rich, he would have to leave home, and he wanted to decide what to do and plan how to leave, and think about where he would go. And he wanted to enjoy the pleasure of considering richness alone, and he felt it could not possibly be shared, this new pleasure, and he was very excited.

The boy with no eyes said he quite understood. He said being rich was exciting, and Youngest Son had many plans to prepare and should be on his own. He said that he'd sit by the road, and he'd wait, and Youngest Son said that he'd pick up their things and come back and they could go off together.

And because he was feeling so light and excited, he threw the market money into the air, just as the boy with no eyes had done, and it fell in the road, and he laughed again and said what did it matter if the money was lost. He was going to have a thousand times more money than that little bit!

The boy with no eyes sat by the side of the road and said that he'd wait and told Youngest Son not to be long, and Youngest Son walked home and tried to plan how he was going to leave without being stopped by Basketweaver and Old Woman.

Back at home, Basketweaver was in the usual place down by the river, working with some new canes. But he was not thinking of his baskets very much. He was thinking of what Old Woman had said concerning the boy with no eyes and the thing that had happened to him concerning the boy with no eyes, and he was trying to understand it all.

A sound came into his ears, and he knew from the sound that the westels were about, and he stopped his work and looked sharply into the water, and he sat very still for a while, listening to the sound of the westels and watching to see what could be seen.

A westel appeared. It came to the surface of the water, but it would not come out of the water.

'There is little time,' said the westel. 'Listen to my story. There is a wicked creature in the land. The wicked creature disguises itself in many forms. It is the great spoiler of the land. It is the enemy of the king. It is our enemy too. The wicked creature has no eyes. It was maimed in a battle with a tine. In all of its forms, the creature has no eyes!

'I bring you a warning,' said the westel. 'When I came to you before, the enemy was with you. By your side. You must understand. Great danger has come to you. A special danger is upon you!'

The westel went back into the water, quickly and without saying any more. Basketweaver hardly heard all that it said before he got to his feet and began running for the house. And while he ran for the house, he thought of the boy and he could believe that the boy was the enemy of the king and the creatures and of any who cared for the land. And it seemed suddenly plain that the boy was the spoiler in the land and he was angry with himself for not having seen this before, and he was afraid that some terrible thing might have happened to Old Woman, for she was alone in the house. And he remembered the warning of the westel, that a special danger was upon them.

But Old Woman was sitting by the window with her lace and nothing had happened to her. Basketweaver said what had happened, about the wicked enemy and the great danger, and they rushed up the stairs and together they took the few things that belonged to the boy with no eyes and put them straight out, not just out of the house, but out onto the road, right away from them all.

Then they returned and went down past the house to the river, to see if the westel could be found. For they both wanted to know more concerning the special danger that had come upon them, and about the wicked creature who had disguised itself as a boy with no eyes. But the westel did not return, and Basketweaver said that he thought perhaps it was afraid because of the wicked enemy, and he said too that they should get back to the house and wait for Youngest Son to come home, and tell him the warning.

But when they got back to the house, Youngest Son was already there. He had a little bag packed up and his face was black and angry, and they knew straight away that it was he and not they who was in danger, and they wanted to protect him and told him at once about the westel and how the boy with no eyes was no boy, but in fact was the wicked enemy that all creatures feared.

Now, on his way home, Youngest Son had been thinking up plans for getting away without Basketweaver and Old Woman stopping him. And when he came to the place in the road where the belongings of the boy with no eyes had been thrown, he knew how he would leave.

'I saw all the things on the road,' shouted Youngest Son, his face all creased up and angry. 'How could you do such a terrible thing? A boy with no eyes and no family to care for him! Just throwing him out on the road and making wicked stories up about him too! I won't stay here, after you've done such a thing to my friend. Do you know what I think of you? I think you're ugly, both of you, I think you're horrible.'

Youngest Son thought Basketweaver and Old Woman would be hurt by his hard words and start crying, and while they were crying he would pick up his bag and just quietly slip away. But they did not seem to be hurt, and there certainly was no crying. They just explained once again, very clearly and with much urgency and emphasis, that the boy with no eyes was no boy but the wicked creature in the land, and they repeated the warning of the westel.

Youngest Son picked up his bag and walked out. Basketweaver and Old Woman did not stop him going. They had given him the warning, but they had seen all the blackness in his face and they knew that he had not taken it in, and they knew he would go, and there could be no stopping him. But they hoped that one day he would remember the warning they had given him.

And so Youngest Son left home. He went off down the road and gathered up the belongings of the boy with no eyes. He came to the place where the boy was waiting and gave him his things, and told him the stupid warning that Basketweaver and Old Woman had given, and they went off together. Youngest Son was happy enough.

After some time, when they had gone quite a way through the land, they came to a crossing in the roads. One road led down along the valley to the place where the orchards were, and one road was the way that they had come. One road led up to the southern hill where the wheat was all swinging about in the sun and the wind, and the last road led up to the dark hill.

'We part ways here,' said the boy with no eyes. 'Which way will you go?' And he himself turned to the road that led up to the dark hill.

Youngest Son thought about going on with the boy, but the dark hill looked like a very barren place, and not at all the sort of place where he would become rich.

'I'll go to the orchards,' he said, 'that seems quite a good place to start getting rich, don't you think?'

He laughed out aloud. It was a fine day and he was feeling very pleased with himself. He made all his thanks to the boy with no eyes, and said that he intended to take his advice and see how it worked. 'Hey,' he said, 'I'll come and look for you, when I'm a rich man. We can have some really good times together.'

The boy with no eyes smiled quietly. 'Now don't worry

about that,' he said, 'I'll probably come looking for you when you're rich.'

They banged each other upon the back and made their farewells. Youngest Son went on to the orchards. The boy with no eyes turned himself to the dark hill.

'It will not be hard to find you,' he said to himself, and with these last words, he went up to the hill.

Seven

KING GERALD TELLS SOME STORIES

One day, King Gerald called fleetings from the land to come to him in his palace. For King Gerald knew that the troubles of the land pressed very hard upon the creatures, and he knew that they despaired and grew tired of waiting for him to come back into the land. And he knew, too, that the creatures thought that their affairs were no longer known to him, far away in his palace, and that they longed for him to return and make a very grand entry, and to make this entry soon and end all their troubles.

'I have some stories to tell you,' said King Gerald to the fleetings, and he gathered them around him. And this was King Gerald's first story.

There was a woman, and she was known as the miller's wife Maud. She was very old and she was very lonely. She lived at the place where the wild wood came down to the valley and she lived in an old miller's cottage with a mill built into the end of it and with the big, wide valley in front of her and the wild wood behind and brambles and all sorts of growing things creeping out of the wood and right over her cottage.

When she was young, the miller's wife Maud was very bright and pretty and gay, and people were always coming for the miller to grind up their grain and to see his wife Maud.

And the miller's wife Maud knew the story of the land. She knew how it had been spoiled and she knew about the good creatures and the wicked enemy, and all the things that had happened. And like all those people who knew these things, she waited for the day when the land and all things in it would be made good again.

One day, the miller died. And then nobody came up the track and the miller's wife Maud lived alone. She had a few pigs and some chickens and she knew how to catch rabbits and she planted potatoes and dug up old roots and she managed quite well, but as the years passed, she grew very bitter that people no longer came visiting her. And the cottage fell into its state of ruin and the wild wood just grew right around it. And the miller's wife Maud cared about nothing and nobody, not even herself.

Then a man came out of the wild wood. The man was a magic maker and he could do magic spells, but the miller's wife Maud didn't know about this. She was only too pleased for his company, and the man, for his part, thought the lonely old mill a good place to stay and do magic, and he stayed and it was not till he'd been in the cottage some time that the miller's wife Maud found him doing his spells.

Now all people were afraid of magic and spells. And when Maud found the man making spells she was greatly afraid. For she knew, and not all people knew, that spells were the device of the wicked enemy, and that anybody doing the spells was the friend of the enemy.

So, when Maud found the man making spells, she told him to go. But the man would not go. Then she knew she should go, if the man would not go, but the cottage was full of old memories of when she was young and of the miller, her husband. She had lived many years on her own in the cottage, and as hard as she tried, the miller's wife Maud could not go.

So she stayed in the cottage and the man who made magic stayed too. And the man did his spells, and the miller's wife Maud kept away from him, as much as she could. Sometimes cotties would pass by her door and warn her to leave, and Maud would say yes, she must go, but she never did go. She remained in her cottage with the man who did spells.

Then King Gerald told a second story.

There were some very fine people who lived in a town. They were snazzy and smart and they liked new-fangled things, and they were all very young and extremely fashionable. Among them were Arthur and Edith.

When October came round, Arthur and Edith decided to marry. They hired a carriage and horses and their friends in the town did the same, and they all drove out into the countryside. They made a most excellent company too, driving along in all their fine clothes, and they were headed by Arthur and Edith, the bride and the bridegroom.

It was early in the morning, a time of the day that had become very fashionable for marrying. The company came to a very fine tree just set back from their path through the fields. It stood on its own in a very lonely place with nothing around, except fields and the company of carriages and the guests and the bride and the groom.

'Oh,' cried out Edith from inside her veil, 'can we stop here?'

And Arthur, who thought her the most splendid of women, said yes, they could, and what a good idea to stop here. So they all drove up to the tree—and with the mists all around them and standing underneath the very fine tree, Arthur and Edith were wed.

When they were wed and the sun had come out from the mists, all the smart, snazzy people, and the bride and the bridegroom, piled back into their carriages and drove back to the town in order to feast the occasion.

And when they got back to the town, they were all quite relieved. For the countryside was very pretty and all right for a quick little journey, but it was such a strange place and the air was so strong that they all felt quite ill from it, and the landscape was bleak and quite boring after a while, and the people were different, and there seemed little comfort at all.

Only Edith was not sure about all this. She had been rather taken by the pretty little trees and the simple country people and the fields and the little animals in the distance. And she liked all the mist and the dew on the grass, and she had been quite impressed by that very fine tree under which they were wed. And she resolved to tell Arthur some time that a smart little house in the country, if it had a few comforts, would be just the thing. As long as they had a good carriage and some horses to get them about, and as long as their friends came to see them, of course.

Then King Gerald told a third story.

There was a young woman and she was carrying a child and the child was soon to be born. This young woman was married to a man who was several years older than herself, and he was the finest and most honourable and upright of men, and he was respected by all the people who knew him because of his knowledge and his learning and his good commonsense. And the only person who did not respect him was the young woman, his wife, who was going to give birth to his child.

Now the young woman was very gay and frivolous and simple. She enjoyed walking on the southern hill and going about in the land. And she loved the good things that she saw, and she was much taken to giggling and laughing a lot, and she liked dancing and singing and making music. She had little time for sitting around making clever conversation and for being too quiet for too long, and for thinking before acting, and reading and learning and writing and trying to be wise. She had never been able to read till she married her husband, and she wished that she never had learned how to read, because she was expected to read all the time, and have opinions as well on the most boring of things. For her husband told her that life was a very serious matter, and the young woman could not take life seriously. She thought it a very light, happy thing. And it seemed that there could be no harmony between them.

One day, while she was carrying her first child and when it was soon to be born, the young woman ran straight out of the cottage where they lived, and left her old husband. She went up the southern hill, and a hard time she had climbing up its steep slopes, because of the child that was soon to be born. And she slept overnight on the hill, with nothing for covering, for she was a very impetuous young woman and she had not planned to leave and she had taken nothing with her.

Her husband came after her in the coldness of the night, and he found her asleep, and he wrapped her all about in warm clothing, and when she turned over and woke up, he was there.

'Now can you see how foolish you are?' said her husband. 'You would be dead with the cold by this time, and your child dead inside you, if I hadn't come after you!'

And he said that she was free to come home and he would never mention the matter again, only she must mend her foolish ways and be a good wife and try to be more thoughtful about things, and serious too instead of frivolous.

The young woman could see that she could well have died in the night with the cold. And she thought that her husband was right, that she was very frivolous and silly. And she said she would come home, and promised to mend her bad ways. And she went home with her husband. She became a good wife to him and respected him, just as the other people who knew him respected him.

The woman bore many children to her husband. But the first of her children, the one that she carried when she ran away to the southern hill when she was young, was a girl, and the girl was called Esther.

'These are my stories,' said King Gerald when the telling was over.

But the fleetings were confused, and they said that they weren't stories at all, but mysteries. For they could not understand why King Gerald had chosen to tell them these things.

King Gerald got up, and he stood before the fleetings and he spoke very plainly and clearly to them.

'Now fleetings,' he said, 'listen very carefully. I cannot tell you the time when I shall come back into the land to make it a good place. But I give you these stories.

'The miller's wife Maud will escape from the man with the spells. The newly wedded couple will give up their town and move out into the land, and something special will happen in the land when they come to it. And the little child, Esther, will learn about me and my enemy and about you and the land, and she will pass these things on, and she will die. All these things will take place, before I come.'

King Gerald smiled. 'Do not think I know nothing of what happens and will happen in the future in the land,' he told the fleetings. 'I know everything.' Then he had said all he wanted to say, and he dismissed the fleetings and he left them, and the fleetings went away from the palace and back to the land, and as they went, they thought about the stories King Gerald had told them. When they came into the land, they searched all about in the wild wood for the miller's wife Maud, for she was the first of the stories, and they wanted to see if it was as King Gerald had said.

It took quite some searching, but they found the old mill cottage, with the wild wood growing over it. And it was a very desolate place, very dark and wild and ruined. The fleetings hid in the wild wood and hoped to see the miller's wife Maud, but she did not appear and it grew dark.

A man suddenly appeared, and the fleetings knew that it was the magic maker. He threw open the mill door and came out of the mill and he shut the door behind him and made off in the dark along the side of the cottage, and he found his way to the cottage door and let himself in. After that, there was darkness and silence again.

Now, the fleetings had seen that it was as King Gerald had said, and they were ready to go, when the door of the cottage was opened again, but very quietly this time, and a woman appeared. She was very bright in the darkness because she was wearing a white nightdress. The fleetings sat still and looked at the woman. She was old, and they knew straight away who she was, and she went away from the cottage very quickly, and straight into the wild wood. Her hair was all loose round her face, and she was not at all dressed for the wild wood, but she went into it without hesitation, and the fleetings just followed her.

The woman climbed up the wild wood for quite a good way. She climbed at great speed, although not without difficulty, but she was old and she soon became tired, and she cried to herself as she climbed, but she never turned round or made any sign of going back.

One of the fleetings came along to her side and stopped her from going on further.

Now the miller's wife Maud knew about fleetings. She

stood in the wild wood with the fleeting before her, and she seemed quite unsurprised at the sight of the fleeting, and she told it her story, very much as King Gerald had told it before.

She said she was leaving the cottage and the spell-making man, and she said that she was in a very great hurry and must get as far away as she possibly could before the spell-maker discovered she had gone, because she was afraid of what he might do to her, for he was a very wicked man.

Then the fleeting said that it would take the miller's wife Maud very much further away than she could possibly get on her own. And it took the old woman up into its wings, and it flew her away to a distant part of the land, and the fleetings took care of the miller's wife Maud, and left her with people who were good and would shelter her.

And when the fleetings were alone altogether, they marvelled that this thing had taken place, just as King Gerald had said. And King Gerald still knew, in his palace far away, what took place in the land and what would happen in the future.

They told all the creatures what King Gerald had said and about the miller's wife Maud, and then they all were full of excitement at the thought that King Gerald still knew what took place in the land, and with the thought too that the king might come soon. And they felt the first joy they had known for a very long time.

Eight

THE SPOILING AND THE SAVING OF KING GERALD'S OAK

Four tree cotties lived at the very top of King Gerald's Oak, in the tips of its branches, and four tree cotties lived in its roots. They were the keepers of the Oak, and as such they were the leaders of all the cotties in the land, and they looked after the Oak and cared for it, and they counted it a great privilege to look after it, and they felt a very special tenderness for it, which they did not feel for any other tree in the land.

For King Gerald's Oak wasn't just any old oak tree. It was the centre of the land, and it was the most pure and perfect tree that had ever grown. And King Gerald had made this tree the centre of the land and had kept it lovely and unspoiled all this time. And King Gerald had given it his name.

Birds and little animals lived within the shade of King Gerald's Oak. Cotties lived in the field, beneath its very fine branches. And now people did too. But the people, unlike the creatures, did not know how special and lovely a tree the Oak really was, that it was the centre of the land and an unspoiled thing.

Arthur and Edith, the people were called. They came along from the town in a smart little carriage, and they had a little house built for them right underneath the branches of King Gerald's Oak, and they lived in this place, in their funny new house, a long way from all the other people in the land and their friends from the town, and they caused quite a stir among the cotties who lived in the Oak and took care of it.

For Arthur and Edith were the sort of people who spoiled whatever they touched and made chaos out of whatever was ordered and lovely. And people had never before lived so close to the Oak and the cotties who cared for the Oak were afraid of what they would do to it.

So the keepers of King Gerald's Oak held a solemn meeting. They looked out at Arthur and Edith's funny little house and at the vegetable garden they had made where the vegetables were wilting away, and they thought about their precious, unspoiled Oak, and were really afraid of what might happen with Arthur and Edith so close.

In the end, the cotties called for the fleetings to help them, and they sent the fleetings away to King Gerald to ask about the people who lived under the Oak, and what should be done about them. For the creatures remembered how King Gerald had cared for this tree and given it his name and kept it from spoiling, and they thought it a matter for him to decide what should be done.

The fleetings went away, and when they returned, it was with the message, 'Don't worry. King Gerald's Oak is a perfect tree and the people can't spoil it.'

There was a great surging about of cotties and a rushing up and down and a flapping around.

'What do you mean?' said the cotties. 'Don't worry! Did King Gerald say that?'

King Gerald had said that, and greatly did it seem to confuse the cotties. They took the fleetings to where King Gerald's Oak was supposed to be growing out of the ground. And when they came to that place, they all began crying. For there, on its side, lay the Oak, its roots sucked clean out of the ground, all chopped up ready for firewood. And they all stood round the hole in the ground where the roots had once been, and they all cried, and they all went up to the Oak in its little pieces, and gently touched the little pieces and cried all the more. And then the fleetings were confused too, and they were all sad together.

Now, Arthur and Edith had found a drawback to their little new house. They had come to the country to grow things, to have vegetables and fruit and fresh flowers of their own, and to live like the country people did. And because they were town people and foolish and knew little of the ways in which things grow, nothing they planted survived, and everything withered away.

This rather upset Arthur, who cared that these lovely fresh things were all dying, and it made Edith cross, for she was sure that their town friends would come visiting and see their lack of success and go away laughing at their efforts to live on the land like the country people did. And Edith blamed Arthur for doing things wrong, and the gardens around them became the cause of great bitterness and misery.

Now the cotties who lived in the Oak knew nothing about this. The first sign of trouble as far as they were concerned was one day when a carriage came by. It was heavily curtained at the windows, and black, and the cotties were frightened when they looked at the carriage, and they didn't know why. The carriage stopped by Arthur and Edith's garden and they put down their work and went up and talked to the person inside through the tiniest crack in the curtain. After some minutes of talking, they jumped inside and drove away.

Some time later, Arthur and Edith returned, alone and on foot. They went straight to the Oak and sprinkled some stuff from a bottle on the ground round the Oak, and in hardly any time the tree just seized up on itself, like a man in great pain, and fell down on its side, and its roots came clean out of the ground. And when it lay there, Arthur and Edith came rushing out in great joy and Arthur chopped it up into little bits for firewood, and Edith said, 'There now, perhaps things will start growing at last. Perhaps the soil will have some goodness for us at last.' And they hastily started planting new vegetables and flowers all around them in the garden, marvelling all the time at how wonderful the soil was going to be now that the horrid tree which had taken away all the goodness had been removed.

This was the story that the cotties told the fleetings. And when they heard it, the fleetings were amazed. For they remembered how King Gerald had said that the people could not spoil the tree. And now King Gerald's Oak was spoiled beyond repair.

They told the cotties to look after the pieces of the Oak, and not to worry, and they went straight back to King

Gerald's palace, as fast as they could, to find out what he had to say about all this. But King Gerald was not to be found, and the gateway to the palace was barred, and the whole palace seemed to be in darkness, and the fleetings could gain no entrance.

They wondered if King Gerald was away from his palace, and they spent a day of searching, but they could not find him at all, and at the end of the day, the fleetings gathered on a mountain top to decide what was to be done, and they were tired and desperate and confused, and they were a very great host. Any creature or person in the land who would have seen them would have marvelled at the sight, for it was a very long time since so many fleetings had gathered together in one place. Now, this great gathering of fleetings decided to split up into companies. One company would try again to find King Gerald. Another company would seek out the sad westels in their homes beneath the water and see if they knew anything about the things that had taken place. And the other company, the bravest of all the fleetings, would go even deeper. This company would go into the darkness beneath the earth and see if it could find even one tine who could tell them something about what was happening. For in these later times, the tines had gone very deep underground, and they were never to be seen any more, and all over the land it was almost as though they no longer existed.

So the fleetings rested themselves overnight. And the next day they set off as arranged. One company took itself through the blue sky to the palace of the king. But the palace was still in darkness, and black cloths were hung from every window, and the gateway was barred and there was nobody to be seen.

Another company flew across the waters all through the day. This company heard the cry of the westels, the saddest cry in all the land, but they could not find the water creatures, and the cry filled them all with great sorrow, for they knew that the westels were mourning for them all. And the fleetings went away with black, heavy hearts and they could not cry because the crying had been done for them. And this was a company of great sorrow.

The third company went into the dark caves beneath the land. They went very deep and this was a terrible thing for the creatures of the air and the sunlight to have to do. But they had become messengers without a king, and they were from a land that had lost its centre, and this gave them a kind of desperate bravery, and so they went deeper and deeper, and darker and still darker, and they came to a darkness which is darker than pitch black, for under the earth there is such a darkness.

And there, in that darkness, one of their company found a tine, a tall, proud tine, once a dweller in the land, a wise one in the land, but now driven deep by the people who destroyed everything that they touched, and by the creature in the land who was the wicked enemy of the king and the greatest spoiler of all.

'Strange things are happening,' said the fleeting to the tine. 'The people have spoiled King Gerald's Oak which is the most perfect tree in the land and the centre of the land, and King Gerald said that this would not be possible. And now King Gerald cannot be found and the tree is destroyed and the king's land has lost its centre.'

'Why have you come to me?' said the tine, and he stood some way apart, with many rocks between himself and the fleeting, because tines were no longer accustomed to contact with other creatures.

'You tines are wise,' said the fleeting, 'and in the dark you know the answers to many secrets. The cotties who keep King Gerald's Oak, and the host of fleetings too, thought that you might know the answer to this mystery.'

Then the tine asked many questions concerning the people and the spoiling of the Oak. Often, as the fleeting spoke, the tine made interruptions because the fleeting spoke very quickly and generally, and the tine said that every little detail was important and must be gone into at length.

When he heard about Arthur and Edith going off in the black carriage and returning with a bottle of some sort of liquid and sprinkling this liquid on the ground around the Oak, and when he heard that the Oak had seized up and fallen over and come right out of the ground as a result of all this, the tine made the fleeting stop its story again, and he wanted to know who the black carriage belonged to and where the people had gone in order to procure such a liquid. And when the fleeting didn't know these things, the tine became very cross.

'You come all this way down into these places,' he said, 'and yet you do not bother to bring a full story with you! You creatures are silly and careless! How can I help you, how can any of we tines help you, unless we know all that there is to be known? Do you not think it important to know where this bottle of liquid came from?'

The fleeting replied that the creatures had not thought too much about this matter, and that it only seemed a little thing, compared to the fact that King Gerald's Oak had been spoiled and the land had lost its centre.

'If King Gerald's Oak has been spoiled when King Gerald said that it would not be,' said the tine, 'then there is no such thing as a little thing. This matter of the liquid is very important indeed. The people would not know how to make such a liquid themselves, you can be sure about that. They could not spoil and ruin the Oak on their own. You must find out where they went in this carriage. You must find out if the king's wicked enemy had any hand in all this. Until we know this, there is no further advice or encouragement or help we can give you.'

Then the tine went away, and the fleeting went away, and it called all the other fleetings out of the dark caves and said what had taken place, and the whole company flew back to the mountain top and met again with the other companies, and it was night time.

The companies reported all that had taken place, and in the morning, they all went back to the cotties, and they told the cotties about the tine in the dark places, and how he had said that Arthur and Edith had maybe been given the special liquid by the king's wicked enemy, and that it was very important to find out if this was so, or else the tine could not help them at all.

So the cotties and the fleetings went about in the land, and they tried to discover where Arthur and Edith had gone in the carriage. They followed the carriage tracks across the fields for as far as they were clear, and then they tried asking country people on the roads if they had seen a black heavy-curtained carriage passing by. And some people did not see the creatures or hear what they said, and other people did see them and hear them, and very helpful these people were too.

But a time came when there were no people to ask, and the creatures were in a lonely wooded copse, and they were tired and thought that they never would find out where Arthur and Edith had gone. They asked the trees to help them, and the trees all bowed in one direction, and the creatures took that direction, and it led them out of the copse and on into pasture land, and then there were no more trees to direct them. Then they asked the pastures to help them, and the grasses parted this way and that and made a very clear pathway for them to pass along. And they passed along the pathway and came to a field in the middle of the pasture land. And this field contained a very smart little shop and nothing else at all, except grass, and the grasses parted one way and the other so that the pathway led right up to the shop, and the smart little shop bore a sign on its front which said TREE SPECIALIST.

Well, the creatures just looked at this shop and they looked at the sign hanging over it, and they were afraid to come anywhere near it. They stood quite a time looking at it, and the cotties would have been surging about in a panic but they were too scared to move, and the fleetings would have flown right away, but they were too scared to move as well.

For they did not believe that a tree specialist lived or worked in this place. They were full of bad feelings, and an ordinary little tree specialist would not have given them such bad feelings.

Eventually, the fleetings stopped thinking about how scared they had become. They remembered that the land had lost its centre and that King Gerald could not be found and that the Oak had been spoiled when he had said that it would not be spoiled, and they remembered that they had to find out all about whoever had given the people the little bottle of liquid with which they had destroyed the Oak, or else the tines could not help them at all.

So they edged their way towards the smart little shop on its own in the fields. And when they started this manoeuvre, the cotties came up behind them, and in this manner they all made for the shop and they all put brave thoughts in their heads, in order to keep them from running away.

Then they came close to the shop. They came up to its windows, and they crowded around underneath the sign which said TREE SPECIALIST and peered in. It was very much like an ordinary shop. There was a wooden counter and shelves behind the counter, fixed up on either side of it. There were all sorts of bits and pieces set out on the shelves in neat order. The shop had a little front door with a glass window in it, and the sun was shining through the glass window and it all looked very bright and cheerful. There was a little bell set up over the front door and a piece of carpet on the floor inside and some chairs, so that customers could sit down while they were being attended to. All in all, there was nothing out of the ordinary.

But the creatures still felt suspicious and scared and they knew something was wrong with this place. The fleetings led the way round to the back of the shop. And there, at the back, stood a heavy-curtained carriage, big and black. The fleetings looked at the carriage and the cotties came up behind them and they wanted to say 'Yes, that's the carriage, that's the one,' but their voices had gone and they could not speak at all.

The fleetings passed by the carriage and came up to the windows at the back of the shop, and the cotties came behind them. They all looked through the windows. It was very dark inside because there was no sun. They could see a fire-place and cooking things spread all around and all the normal trappings of everyday living. And they saw something else too. On a shelf in a corner, they saw rows of little glass bottles containing some sort of liquid, and they looked at each other knowingly, and nodded to each other and it seemed that this place was very evil and strange, and not at all like the front of the shop.

Then a figure appeared. It was an ordinary shopkeeper figure, but when the creatures saw it, they all froze, and they knew right away from the way that they felt, that they were looking at the king's wicked enemy. And when he turned round from the fire and crossed over the room, they knew from the way that he looked, with no eyes in his head, who he was.

For a minute or two, they seemed unable to move. Then the cotties turned around and ran as fast as they could, and the fleetings flew up in the sky, as fast as they could, and they all got away from that place, and they all knew quite surely how Arthur and Edith had spoiled the Oak.

The cotties went rushing back through the land to where the Oak lay chopped up into pieces for fuel for the sitting-room fire. And the fleetings raced through the sky up to the high hills and the caves which were the entrance to the dark places where the tines lived.

But they didn't need to go deep as before. For when they got to the high hills, and when they came to the caves, they found the tines there, waiting for them. They stood in the mouths of the caves, and they looked very strange, very tall and quiet and all covered right over in great, heavy coverings to protect them from the light. And when the fleetings came, they lifted the coverings and showed themselves to the fleetings, and then, when they had shown themselves, they dropped down the coverings again and stood very upright and when they spoke, it was through the coverings.

The fleetings said that they had discovered where the people had gone, and that it was the wicked enemy of the king who had given them the liquid with which they had spoiled King Gerald's Oak.

The tines stirred very slightly when they heard this, and they were like tall trees swaying in the breeze, and they swayed up together and away from each other again, and they whispered together, much as the wind whispers in the tops of the trees, and they whispered that this was the time after all, this was the time, they had thought it the time, but they had had to make sure.

The fleetings didn't know what it was that they were whispering. They caught little bits of it and they couldn't understand. But they were sure it was all very important, and they were impatient and they called out to the tines to tell them what was happening, and the tines stopped their swaying and whispering and seemed to remember that the fleetings were there again, and they became very still again, and very upright and proud, and they gave the fleetings a message.

'Go back to King Gerald's Oak,' they said. 'Have no fear for the power of the wicked enemy. It has no power compared to the power of King Gerald. This was the last of the great plans of the enemy, to destroy this precious tree, and it has come to nothing.

'King Gerald will take the land back to himself,' said the tines, 'and this is the beginning. This tree is the first spoiled thing in the land that the king will restore and make good. King Gerald is coming very soon. We shall be safe and content in the land as we were in the beginning. We shall be glad very soon!'

And then the tines turned away and went back into the caves without saying anything else, and they melted back into the darkness that is darker than any other thing in the land.

Now, when the fleetings heard these words, that King Gerald was coming very soon, they became very excited and they went up into the sky and they sped back down the high hills and across the southern hill and into the great valley and along the valley to the place where King Gerald's Oak had been, and they came to rest in that place.

They were greeted by a very amazing sight. The field of King Gerald's Oak was full of cotties, all in a state of confusion and rushing about from one end to the other and moving together, never stationary, as though they were afraid of stepping out alone, and afraid of standing still in one place.

For, in the middle of the field, and where it had always been, stood King Gerald's Oak. At least, the form of the Oak was there, for in substance the tree was quite different. It was not a tree of green, sappy leaves and brown, twiggy branches any more, but it was all over a most wonderful silver and it was glorious to look upon and it grew strong, stronger it seemed than before, with roots deeper than ever in the ground, and branches stretching out further than ever in every direction, even over Arthur and Edith's little new house. It was as though it had always been there, it was so big and strong, except that it was now glorious and silver and lovelier than ever before. And as they looked at it, the fleetings remembered the words of the tines that this tree would be the first spoiled thing in the land to be restored.

The fleetings came right up to where the cotties had gathered in a corner of the field. The keepers of King Gerald's Oak separated themselves from the others and came up to the fleetings. They told how this thing had suddenly happened and how every creature was too afraid to go near the tree because none could understand what had happened, and all the time they spoke, they glanced awkwardly all about them, at the Oak and at the ground and up into the sky, as though they were afraid of what would happen next.

Then the fleetings told them about the tines who were waiting for the day when King Gerald would come. And they told them the things that the tines had said.

'We must not be afraid,' they said, 'we must take shelter in the Oak, just like before. The tines from under the earth said that this was a sign that King Gerald would come and take back his land and make it good again. They said that this was the beginning, and that we should be glad for it.'

So the creatures could be glad. But inside their little house, Arthur and Edith had no reason to be glad. They could not see all the things that are to be seen, nor could they understand all the things that there are to be understood. And they certainly could not understand this little bit of it all! Where the field was full of fleetings in all their splendour, they could only see silly old birds, and they worried about the birds coming over and spoiling their newly-planted, precious garden. And they could not see the cotties at all, just a moving about of the grass and they thought it a high wind that made the grass move so much.

They could see King Gerald's Oak, growing as though it had never been felled and chopped up. And much did it confuse and amaze them. But they could not see that it was more glorious than ever and that it was now made of the most wonderful silver. They sat in their parlour and looked out of the window and felt very strange, that the tree should be growing again, and afraid. And for them, there was nothing to rejoice in at all, and they could not be glad.

Out in the field, on the other hand, there was much reason for gladness. The cotties thought about the message from the tines under the earth. And then the keepers of the Oak, as one body and all together, left all the others and marched off to the tree, and the four who had lived at the very top climbed back up to the very top, to the tips of the branches, and the four who had lived in its roots got down again into those roots.

Then all the other cotties, and the fleetings as well, rushed up to the tree, and they greatly loved it, and they danced around it and climbed up into its silver branches and nestled among its silver leaves, and they were very glad.

And in the palace of King Gerald, there was much rejoicing. Down came the black cloths, and the gateway was unbarred once again, and music and laughter and singing and the tap of dancing feet could be heard all through the day and long into the night. Only King Gerald was quiet, and he was preparing himself for the things that were to come.

Nine
ESTHER

There was a family who lived down in the valley at the bottom of the southern hill. This family was made up of mother and dad and Esther who was ill and the twins who were difficult and the boys and the little ones. And the southern hill cotties, and the fleetings too, kept watch over this family because of Esther. For Esther, the oldest daughter, had been mentioned by King Gerald himself, concerning the time when he would return into the land.

Late one afternoon, towards the end of summer, mother and dad and Esther and the twins and the rest of the children went over to Old Lovepace's.

When they came out, the moon had risen and was hanging low over the southern hill. It was full and bright and yellow and filled the lane with shadows. Esther looked about her. The yellow lane and the trees as well were full of cautious, half-hidden cotties, more than she had ever seen before. And she thought that it must be a special night, with so many cotties out.

Old Lovepace shook mother and dad by the hand, nodded briefly at the children and lingered fondly over his farewell with Esther. She was his special favourite and he could see, with his old man's eyes, that the little visit had worn her out and that she was not at all well.

Young Lovepace then shook hands with them all, and offered Esther a ride home in his new motor car, and he made the offer in a big, loud voice so that they could all hear, and then they were all amazed, as no doubt they were supposed to be, because nobody in the valley possessed one of these strange new machines, and they would never have thought anything so modern would have reached them, under the southern hill.

Esther said how exciting it would be to ride home in a motor car, but not tonight thank you, it was such a beautiful, clear night and she'd rather try the walk with the others. Mother and dad fussed around her saying didn't she think if Young Lovepace had a motor car she should go home in it, but Esther refused to pay any attention to mother and dad, and then they got cross with her and still she would pay no attention to them, and in the end they gave up and put her up into the little trap and got everybody into line. Then they all made off down the lane with the Lovepaces waving them goodbye, and they were like some sort of dark, spotted snake, streaming along in black visiting clothes and with straw hats and covered heads bobbing about. And the twins thought they were like the fairy people because the yellow moon had made everything like fairyland and they thought mother and dad were like the king and the queen, tall and majestic in their fine clothes, mother with her red shawl wrapped around her head and dad with his ivory-topped cane. The twins had just found out about these things.

The order in which they walked was the order in which they always walked on family walks. Mother and dad were at the head. The little ones marched behind in a company of varying sizes and speeds. The twins hung back and kept as apart from the others as they could get, and whispered together and wished that they could just go off into the night and have adventures. And Esther was at the very back, sitting quite upright in the little trap, with the pony trotting as slowly as it could be made to trot, and the boys with her, one sitting by her side to give her support, and the other leading the pony and trying to keep the trap from jerking about too much. For the lane was very uneven and Esther was in a lot of pain.

In this way, the little procession came by Five Fallows Pond. And they stopped by Five Fallows Pond and looked at it and thought it a lovely sight, with the southern hill behind and the moon rising above. Some little trick of the moon reflected the moving light and shade of the water onto their faces, and the faces laughed at each other, and the twins said 'Look, magic!' and 'It's a spell!' because that was the way that it made them feel.

'No,' said dad sternly. 'There's no such thing as magic. Now come along and let's get home.'

And the procession got back into line and slithered once again down the lane.

Once home there was all the noise and commotion of everybody rushing around and getting out of their visiting clothes and not having to be well-behaved any more and being allowed to make as much din as they liked. Mother banked up the fire and dad got down a book from the shelf and started reading.

The twins slipped outside. They didn't want to come in out of the yellow moonlight. They felt all caught up in it. Esther and the boys had just arrived. Esther looked very tired and ill, and the boys helped her out of the trap and on to the porch. Mother came out and said that she and dad would carry Esther up to her bed, but she said no, she wanted to sit out. This worried mother who said that this wasn't a good idea at all. Esther had just put a great deal of strain on herself by going visiting when she was so ill, and she ought to be taking more care. And mother said too, that if Young Lovepace had a motor car, Esther was a very silly girl not to have come home in it instead of jogging along the lane in the old trap.

'But think what I would have missed,' said Esther, and she smiled as though the idea of missing the family walk was quite out of the question.

'I'm all right, mother, now you don't have to worry,' she said. 'Just fetch me some covers, and I'll sit out here, right by the door where you can keep an eye on me.'

The twins followed mother indoors. Morgen took the blankets and Morwen assured mother that if she had things to do, they would be very happy to sit out and keep an eye on Esther, and in fact they had intended to sit out anyhow.

Mother looked wistful, as though she would have liked to sit out in the yellow evening herself, but dad called, 'Mother, shouldn't the little ones be going up now?' from the depth of his book, and mother stirred herself and pushed some medicine into Morwen's hand and said that Esther must take some and she told her how much, and

Morwen promised to see to this, and the twins went back out into the yellow summer night and wrapped Esther up in the big, heavy coverings, and wrapped themselves up too, because it was getting colder.

The three of them sat silently together and looked out over the southern hill, watching the journey of the moon. Esther was thinking about the fleetings and about all those cotties in the trees and on the lane. She had known for a long time now that the cotties were watching them, and she thought that it was on her account, but she didn't know why and they never spoke to her about it or came close. And she tried to unfathom all this, as she looked up to the southern hill.

The twins were thinking about magic. They had found a magic book full of fairyland and fairies and witches and wizards and spells and the doing of magic. Well, the twins had dismissed the fairies and fairyland as make-believe for children. But witches and wizards were real people and they had thought a lot about them and a lot too about making spells, and it seemed a very exciting thing to do. And although they did not speak to each other, Morwen and Morgen were both thinking about spells, as they looked at the southern hill, and wondering how they could do them. For the night was yellow and exciting and different, and the strangest feeling wrapped them all about, and they were quite lost in it.

Esther turned away from the southern hill and she looked at the twins and saw the same expression in both their faces, and she thought it rather a strange way for them to be looking, and said, 'What are you thinking about?'

The twins stirred themselves and stared at Esther. They would not, for all that their lives were worth, have dared tell mother or dad what they were thinking about, but Esther was different. If there was such a thing as magic, they could well believe that Esther was a magic person. She was like a creature of the hills and the sky, or a little piece of nature, a gentle piece of nature, and it seemed easy to say, when she asked, 'We're thinking about magic.'

'Ah,' said Esther, and she smiled her lovely smile to herself, 'Tell me about magic then.'

So the twins told her about the book that they had found and about how they had thought that maybe it was possible to do spells and really make magic things happen, and they told her all the things they had considered about this and how they intended to try some things out, and Morwen said that she was considering turning herself into a tree, and Morgen, who didn't want to be left behind on her own, said that she was considering turning herself into a tree too, but by a different method.

'Oh,' said Esther, 'and what methods are you going to use?'

Then the twins admitted that they really didn't know just yet, but they were sure that something would work out if they thought about it long enough. They had only just found out about magic, and it all needed a lot of thought.

'So you think that there might be more things around than you knew about before?' said Esther, and when the twins agreed that this was precisely so, she said, 'Well, let me tell you some things.' And she told the twins about the creatures that lived in the land and that not all people could see, and she told them how, even now, there were cotties all around them, and that for a long time now the cotties, and the fleetings too, had been watching them. And she told these things to whet the twins' appetites so that they would want to hear other things too, and to bring excitement to them.

But the twins were not excited. Rather, they felt extremely awkward when Esther told them these things. They thought that Esther was humouring them and that she had not believed all that they said about magic and that she was just making up some little thing to keep them happy and in order to seem sympathetic and understanding. For the cotties and the other creatures sounded no different to the fairies in fairyland, and the twins had already discarded all that as nonsense.

Esther saw at once that they were awkward and she asked them why, and because she was Esther and so sweet and the sort of person that you could not help but tell the truth to, the twins told her why.

'Oh dear!' said Esther, 'I'm not trying to keep you happy

at all. I'm not even talking about magic things. That's something else altogether, and not such a very good thing either. No, I'm talking about deep truths. I'm talking about things that are mysteries to some but to others are very plain. I'm talking about things that really are all about us, creatures who have been in this land since before people came into it, and creatures who have a wisdom that people will never be able to match.'

Then the twins could see that Esther was not humouring them after all and that she was very serious in all that she said. But they could not understand the things that she spoke about, and they asked her to say more.

'Those of us for whom these things are plain are like a great family of people who have been chosen and are special,' said Esther. 'Perhaps you are chosen. Perhaps these things will be plain to you.'

And she proceeded to tell them many stories, about how people had come into the land and how the land had a king, King Gerald, and how King Gerald had an enemy in the land who was a very wicked creature, and how one day King Gerald was going to come back into the land to make all things good.

'Look at the southern hill,' said Esther, 'and look at me. We're both groaning and moaning in our different ways. We're both spoiled, you know. But when King Gerald comes, we won't be like this. I'll go walking up on the southern hill again and it'll be a beautiful southern hill because King Gerald will have made it beautiful, and I'll be quite well again, because King Gerald will have made me well.'

And she told many other things besides, and all the time she explained the things that she said, so as to make them as clear as possible. And her stories were wonderful and exciting and she kept saying that this was not magic, this was something else, and the twins got all excited and thought it a wonderful thing that there was a King Gerald, and that all these things were so, just as Esther was saying.

'Oh,' said Morgan, 'Oh Esther! Whoever told you all these things? Esther, how did you ever come to find it all out?' For this seemed to make everything in life different for ever, it was so wonderful and so huge and amazing.

Esther leaned back in her chair, and they could see that the long conversation and all the story-telling was tiring her and that she was unwell, and they were thinking that perhaps they should go away and then she could tell them some more another day, when Esther said, 'Old Lovepace told me these things. And when I heard them, I went about in the land seeking out the creatures and the signs that what he said was true, and I found that it was true, just as Old Lovepace told it to me.'

There was a silence. Suddenly, everything was awful. The twins' excitement just drained out of them, just went right away. They were very still and they felt a little bit as though they had been kicked good and hard, with a dreadful feeling inside of their stomachs, and they just stared at each other and then at Esther, and they didn't know what to say.

Esther, leaning back in her chair, saw all this in the twins' faces. 'Old Lovepace is a very good man,' she said firmly, 'you should get to know him a bit, talk to him.' And she wanted to say more, but she was exhausted and she just stared off at the southern hill.

'Esther,' said Morwen, 'why haven't any other people except you and Old Lovepace seen these things, the creatures that you told us about? Why don't all people know about them?'

Esther turned her head slightly. 'Not all people are chosen,' she said. 'The people who go looking for the creatures and the people who believe the stories when they are told them are chosen people in the land.'

'Esther,' said Morgen, 'if we go and look for these creatures, will we find them?'

'If you go looking,' said Esther, 'you'll find them. Yes, you will. You'll find them.'

And then she would say no more because she was very ill and very tired. The twins were ashamed of themselves for tiring her so. They were also full of sad feelings, for no matter what Esther said, it had only come from Old Lovepace after all and they could not believe it.

They crept indoors and told mother how tired Esther had

become, and then they went on upstairs, and all the excitement had quite gone out of them, and they could only remember Old Lovepace's silly face as they had seen it only today, and they just kept wondering how Esther could possibly believe anything that Old Lovepace had told her. And yet they could not forget the stories that Esther had told them, because they were the most beautiful stories they had ever heard, and they could not help themselves from wishing that they were true.

Mother went out to Esther and said that she would take her in. Esther opened her eyes and she looked like a very old woman just for a minute, and mother went quite pale when she looked at her, but then Esther smiled her lovely smile and she looked young and like Esther again. She parted her lips ever so slightly and whispered to mother please to leave her alone, she wanted to stay looking at the southern hill. And mother knew that the sensible thing was to take her in and put her to bed, and that was what dad would have done if he had come out, but she smiled softly at her first child, and for a moment it was as if there was something between them, and then she came indoors again and left Esther alone to look at the southern hill.

The twins went to bed. With their heads full of Esther, and with the bright yellow moon streaming into the bedroom and the noise of the little ones tossing about, they tried to sleep and lay side by side and could not sleep at all.

They whispered to each other, about the king and the creatures, and a couple of times Morgen got up on the bed and stretched herself out towards the window ledge and peeped out to see if perhaps there were creatures there, because Esther had said that if they looked, they would quite surely find the creatures. But Morwen said that she was wasting her time, all this stuff came from Old Lovepace and couldn't possibly be true, and even if it were true, Esther had said that only chosen people would see things, and she said that magic was much better than that because magic could be for anyone who cared to find out about it. Morgen got back into bed and said that perhaps it was all because Esther was so ill, perhaps when she was better she wouldn't believe these things. And in this way, still mumbling to each other, the twins fell into a state of half sleep.

After some time, there was a lot of noise downstairs, mother calling to dad, running around, and footsteps on the stairs, and then mother's voice next door telling one of the boys to get dressed quick and go for the doctor.

The twins got out of bed and the little ones began to wake up and they all poured out onto the landing and down the stairs, rubbing their eyes and moaning and asking what was wrong. And at the bottom of the stairs and by the front door and in her chair, wrapped up in the covers that the twins had tucked around her, Esther sat, dead.

The little ones screamed and cried, and mother, who was crying quietly anyhow, cried all the more. She bundled them all back upstairs and tried to say comforting things to them, and she still cried all the more. Dad wrapped Esther right over with the covers and after a bit the doctor came and said that there was nothing that could have been done.

The twins crept away down the leering yellow garden and were sick together in the vegetable patch and lay out there all night, huddled together for comfort and trying to take in what death was all about, and crying a great deal. Esther had been there. She had been real, just a few hours ago. Now she was dead. It wasn't the ugliness of a dead person that kept them out all night. It was the ugliness of death itself.

In the morning, dad came out and woke them up and said that they should come indoors, and perhaps even go to bed, and the little ones came out and stood around him. The twins thought how tall and grand he looked, beside the little ones, and how last night they had thought that he and mother looked like the fairy king and queen, and then dad had said there's no such thing as magic, and then Esther had said all that she said.

They went up to bed because it seemed like a good place to be, right out of the way. Morwen thought about Esther and cried and could not sleep. Morgen could not sleep either, but a new thought was filling her head. She was plagued with the idea that Esther perhaps had been right in the things that she said and that there were more real things in the land than she had seen. She even got up to the window to look, but nothing was there.

Morwen fell asleep. But Morgen lay awake all through the day and until evening came. Then she slept too.

Ten

THE PARTING OF MORWEN AND MORGEN

Morwen wanted to become a tree. She went into the wild wood by the waterfall and asked the trees what she should do about it. Nothing happened. She rolled about in the earth and rubbed it into her face and tried to be as unlike a person and like a tree as possible, but when she got up she was still not a tree. She was just a dirty person.

Now Morwen was a wild and unruly young woman, and she would not give up wanting to become a tree. She went down the track to Emily's cottage. Emily's cottage was like a giant green mound with bright eyes where the creepers had been trained round the windows. Emily kept roses out the back and rows of cabbages and potatoes. Inside the cottage she had an amazing plant that her brother had brought from a very distant place. It crept up the wall and across the ceiling and it had started to work its way down the other wall as well, and it was so thick and tangled that in the spring, little birds would fly into the cottage and nest in it. Emily was all that remained of the old world when people were not so civilized and modern, and Morwen thought that perhaps she might know what could be done.

Emily told Morwen that she couldn't be a tree.

'The best you can do is to devote yourself to serving the trees,' she said. 'People are a very humble part of the order of things, you know, but they don't seem to realize it. You can't just expect to be something as important as a tree, you know.'

'But I don't want to serve,' said Morwen, who wanted to be a tree. 'I want to be a tree. I want to live on like the trees do and not die like people do. I mean, people die so fast, don't they? But trees just go on and on, and I want to do that as well.'

'Oh dear, you've quite got the wrong idea,' said Emily. She pottered across the little room and put a kettle on the fire and Morwen watched her and thought that probably not in the whole of her life would she see that again, because people just didn't put kettles on fires any more, and it reminded her of when she was young, and it made her sad. Emily sat down by the fire. She knew nothing about modern people.

'You must serve,' she said. 'And you should be proud of death too. Death is the final service. You shouldn't be afraid to die. It's an honour. You'll be planted back into the earth and the trees will nourish themselves on your body and carry on living because of you. Then you'll be part of every other living thing, because that's what the earth is, so many thousands and millions of dead bodies!'

'I don't want to die,' said Morwen, who wanted to be a tree.

She went away and she met Morgen along the track on the way back home again. Morgen had been out searching for the signs of King Gerald which she believed she would find one day in the land.

'Hello,' Morgen said, 'where have you been?' For when she looked into Morwen's face, she saw things that other people would not have seen there.

Morwen wanted to say where she had been. She wanted Morgen to want all the things that she wanted and to go along with her everywhere she went. But Morgen was growing away from her, faster all the time, and suddenly she felt a need to keep where she had been secret to herself.

So she made up some untrue excuse to explain where she'd been. Morgen knew it was untrue, and was surprised, and Morwen knew that Morgen knew, and they walked home together in silence.

'Where have *you* been then?' Morwen said, as they came to the cottage. And Morgen felt the same sudden inclination to be secretive, as though nothing could be shared between them any more.

'Oh, just along by the stream for a breath of fresh air,'

she said. Then they carried on inside, and went their separate ways among the rest of the family.

Morwen went to see Agnes. Agnes told fortunes, which was the nearest you could get to magic in those days. She had a little parlour at the back of the local shop. It was decked out with black curtains and low lights and she dressed herself up all in black. You weren't allowed to give her money because that was against the law. But if you were grateful, and she hoped you would be, you could leave some little thing with Alfred in the shop.

'I want to be a tree,' Morwen said.

Agnes was quite taken by surprise. Nobody had come to her with that particular request before, and she didn't know what to do. She said a few wise-sounding things and suggested that Morwen should consult the stars to see if it was the right time of the year for such an activity, but Morwen insisted that everything was just right and as it should be, and so Agnes went away and came back with a little glass bottle, like a medicine bottle with an old-fashioned stopper in it, half full of some transparent liquid. She said that if Morwen was sure about becoming a tree, she should drink this. Then she gave her detailed instructions about when to drink it and how to drink it and what to do afterwards. She finished up by saying that if it didn't work, it wasn't her fault or the fault of the liquid, but that it must be the wrong time with the stars after all.

Morwen left Agnes and the shop. She gave something to Alfred on the way out, not because she was grateful but because like most people, she cared about what they would think of her if she didn't. But she threw the little bottle away as soon as she possibly could, because she realized that the liquid was probably no more than plain old sugar-and-water, and she knew now that Agnes couldn't really help her, and she thought how foolish she had been to go there in the first place.

Morwen and Morgen lay in bed in the dark. The moon was hidden by clouds. There were no stars. There was no light across the land. It was all shadows. And quite awake, with their eyes both wide open, Morwen and Morgen were like two strange dreamers among all the shadows.

Morgen got out of bed and began to dress. Morwen sat up in bed and watched her while she dressed. Morgen finished getting ready and she went around the side of the bed and stood by Morwen's side, and Morwen and Morgen looked at each other.

'Morwen,' said Morgen, 'Morwen, I'm going outside. Will you come with me?'

Morwen looked very hard and very sad as well. 'I want to be a tree,' she said. 'Come with me into the wild wood.'

'You know where I'm going,' Morgen said. 'Come with me.'

'I want none of it,' Morwen said, and she closed her eyes so that she no longer looked at Morgen. Then Morgen went away from her and across the room and out of the door, and it was the final parting, the parting that had come to them slowly, all through the years of their childhood and right until now. She went out of the room and left Morwen alone.

Morgen crept through the house. She thought of going back, but the faint little song of the westels, the sound that had woken them both in the dark, was growing stronger, and she would not go back. She went down the stairs and let herself out, very quietly, and the song of the westels swelled loud and fell soft. Morgen stepped out into the song.

Morwen heard the song swelling and fading. Her face was like stone. She turned on to her side after Morgen had gone, and she thought about the trees in the wild wood and wanted nothing at all but to join them.

She went back down to the wild wood by the waterfall and pleaded with the trees to take her in.

The wild wood was a place where nature seemed to be arrayed in its most decadent glory. Everything grew off everything else, plants were strangled by plants, insects preyed on each other and tree fought against tree in an attempt to be the highest and the one that reached the sunlight far above them all. The wild wood was very dark and very dense and very quiet and it was not a place for people at all. And this excited Morwen, and she rushed up and down saying, 'I want to join you, I want to join you, I want to join you,' and she rolled down the last steep incline and right on to a log that hung like a bridge over the stream. She lay face down on the log and watched the stream moving underneath her and watched the spiders hanging on their webs, and she listened to the waterfall behind her, and said, 'Please take me in.'

Everything remained just as it was and Morwen noticed neither sound nor movement to suggest that she had been heard at all.

'Look,' she whispered into the log, with her lips right up against its bark. 'You're my only hope. I don't want to be a terrible person any more. Really, I don't. I want to be a tree like you.

'Please,' said Morwen to the log, 'Say something to me.'

Now Morwen was not alone in the wild wood, for a fleeting was there too and it had watched her progress down that last sloping incline to the stream and had heard the words that she whispered to the log as she lay on it. The fleeting came out from among the trees and down towards Morwen, and she lifted her head and stared at the creature. It was very beautiful and very white and it was quite amazing. It came right down close beside Morwen, and she stayed lying on the log with her head lifted up a little bit, and only one thought was in her head and that was that this creature would have powers different from those of people, and perhaps it could make her into a tree.

The fleeting introduced itself as a messenger of King Gerald and an inhabitant of the land.

'You waste your time in waiting for the trees to talk to you,' it said, 'the trees can't talk to you. Don't you know that people are more than trees because they can talk and feel and trees cannot. All trees can do is grow.'

Morwen just stared at the fleeting and she hated it for saying that people were more than trees. For she had seen that people were terrible things, and her admiration for the trees was very great indeed.

'I don't believe you,' she said, and she lay her face on the log and it was her dear friend and she felt safe and protected to be so close to it, and she had no qualms at all

about disagreeing with such an amazing creature who was a messenger of King Gerald. 'Trees have a different language from us,' she said, 'and we can't understand them. When I say something, I know they reply. I know they do. It's just that I can't understand yet.'

'A bird without wings cannot fly,' said the fleeting mysteriously. 'Trees have no hearts.'

Morwen pulled herself away from her log and sat quite upright. She had time for only one thing, and the time pressed upon her.

'I just want to be a tree,' she said. 'I don't really care what you say. I don't like being a person and I want to change what I am.'

The fleeting spoke very gently. 'People have been placed over the trees as lords of the trees,' it said. 'Don't you know you are more than the trees?'

'I don't care!' said Morwen, and she was very impatient because she was sure that this amazing creature could turn her into a tree or do any other thing that she asked it, and she wanted to be a tree very quickly and very soon.

'Look,' she said. 'It's quite simple. When I look at the trees with their feet all down in the earth and their heads up high in the sky, I want to be one of them. When I look at people, I don't want to be one of them. People are dreadful. Do you know, out here in the wood I stand apart from everything else because I'm a person and that means I'm dreadful. I don't want it to be like that. I want to be a tree, and I want to belong and I don't want to stand apart any more.'

'There is something more I must tell you then. You must listen to what I say,' said the fleeting. And the fleeting told Morwen the story of King Gerald and the land, and how people had come into the land and been spoilers. It told Morwen that King Gerald would come back into the land and would give people a loveliness that no other thing possessed. And the fleeting said that the reason why people stood apart wasn't because of their dreadfulness, but because they were special. King Gerald loved people more than trees, and he would bring a gladness among the people if only they would wait for it, and this gladness would be unlike anything that the trees would ever know.

Morwen listened quietly to these things, sitting upright on her log, and she was quite, quite sure that all these things were true and exactly as the fleeting told them. But Morwen didn't care about them at all. She didn't care for the waiting, nor did she care for the gladness, nor did she care for King Gerald.

'I wouldn't want to be glad if the trees weren't glad with me,' she said. 'No matter what happens, the trees will be best in my eyes. I want to be a tree, not a person.'

'Trees will have their last days,' said the fleeting. 'Just as the land will have its last days, at the end. But people will go on beyond the end.'

Morwen laughed. 'Imagine the trees having last days,' she said. 'Just look how strong and secure they are! Anyhow, I wouldn't want to go on, if the trees did have last days and were no more.'

The fleeting was very sad. 'Then you shall be a tree,' it said. 'For as long as the land remains. And when the end days are over, you will be nothing.'

And so Morwen became a tree. Birds nested in her branches and sometimes cotties built their homes down in her roots. Morgen passed her by, seeking out her sister whom she had lost, and Morgen never knew what she had passed, and she went away, far from the southern hill.

And Morwen stood on, silent, long after Morgen had passed her and gone away. You could see her, if you could find her, down in the wild wood by the waterfall. She grows somewhere close to that old log over the stream. Her roots are full of her life and they dig deep into the earth, and she will live like that for as long as the land lives. One day, King Gerald will come just as the fleeting said, and he will make people lovely, and at that time Morwen and all the trees will become beautiful too, more beautiful than words can describe. But in the end days, when all things are over, the trees will be no more and the people will go on and on. For trees belong to the season. They are taken on by time from new leaves to old, gentle green to bare blackness. Springtime and autumn. In the wild wood by the waterfall, nothing lasts beyond the season.

She knows now, Morwen who has lost her heart, that people are above the trees. She knows the secrets that people can't see. Down in the wild wood by the waterfall, the ones without hearts know the king of the land. And they know that it is the people, not they, who are his special joy and who will last beyond the season.

Eleven

MORGEN MEETS KING GERALD

Morgen was going home. She woke up in her little bedroom in the town and it was four o'clock in the morning. She turned over in the bed and sighed and went through all the motions of falling back to sleep, but she didn't fall back to sleep. Five minutes later she was still wide awake, and no amount of deep breathing and sighing would make any difference. There was a little bubble of excitement inside her and it kept her awake and it kept her head lively and clear, and she was anxious for it to be light and for the day to begin so that she could be off.

She closed her eyes tightly and tried to drift to sleep. She thought about home. She thought about the southern hill and the woods and the twists in the lanes and the cottages and their cottage, and she thought about mother and dad at their cottage. She thought about the sky and the soft, loose-limbed clouds that used to hang sometimes over the southern hill, and she tried to drift along on a soft, loose-limbed cloud of her own, until sleep took her off.

But sleep didn't take her off, and in the end she gave up attempting to sleep and sat up in bed and wrapped a cover round her shoulders and resigned herself to staring at the walls and watching the day as it came. And she bubbled with excitement that she couldn't keep down, and she wished that the morning would hurry and come and she could be on her way.

While she was sitting like this, the strangest little feeling came to Morgen. It was strange because it was altogether different from her excitement, and because it came very suddenly. It was as if something were going to happen, something very special. And as she had nothing else to look forward to, Morgen thought that it must be because she was going home.

But the feeling was so different from anything before. And when it had gone, quickly and much as it came, it left her puzzled. She wondered if there was some other thing after all that she was meant to be looking forward to and that she had forgotten about. And she spent a long time thinking about this, and in the end she decided that there was nothing else, she was sure there was nothing at all.

She got out of bed and decided to wash and get dressed. It seemed silly to sit up in bed quite awake doing nothing. She counted out the hours before she would be home, right to the cottage, and she wondered who among the family would be there to greet her.

She put on her slippers and opened her little packed case by the bed for her washing things, and she'd forgotten the strange little feeling, and she was thinking about home again and being excited again, when something else came to her, suddenly as before. She jumped up and turned round and she was quite sure that she was being watched, that she was not on her own and that something was going on around her.

She looked all about and nothing had changed in the room to give her this feeling, and no one was there. But she still had the feeling that something was happening today and she ought to know what and she couldn't think what, and as though someone was there in the dark.

She told herself that she was being stupid and that her excitement at going home had got the better of her, and in the end she went all round the room and looked into everything closely, and although she still thought she was watched, there was nothing at all.

She went over to the window, the only place in the room that she hadn't examined. She pulled back the curtains to let in the morning and see what was there, and there was nothing at all. There was no secret watcher outside the window or behind the curtains. And there was no morning either, only a mist that hung around in the dark.

Morgen stared at the mist and watched it moving. If she had been at home, the mist would not have surprised her.

But here in the town where they never had mists, Morgen was surprised and the notion that something was happening came to her very much stronger than before.

She sat down by the window ledge and tried to make out the shapes of the other houses and the streets and the roof-tops and chimneys, and she could see none of these things, because the mist was so thick. The lightness of morning came slowly but all Morgen saw was the mist turning white all around her.

Then, just for a second, she thought something was going on underneath that mist, something special and secret, something sudden and strange, as her feelings were sudden and strange. But she shook her head briskly and laughed out aloud at herself and thought it ridiculous that going home should make her excited enough to imagine all these things.

But even when she had laughed out aloud, and when she had quite dismissed any nonsense from out of her head, she remained by the window ledge looking out into the mist, and it was as though she was looking for something within it or waiting for something to happen.

And something did happen, after a while. A creature came out of the mist. Morgen didn't see it at first because the creature was wrapped all about in white covers and out in the mist it just looked like more mist. But the creature came up close and then Morgen saw it. It passed through the window and came into her room and it threw off its covers, and she knew what it was from the signs of its age on its face, and its wisdom, and its height and its pride.

For Morgen knew of the creatures that lived in the land, and this was a tine, a wise one from under the earth. And Morgen knew very surely that something was happening to-day, and something had spread out the mist in the land for a purpose and woken her up and put the strange feelings inside of her, and brought this tine to her from under the earth.

She was brimming with questions and they all tumbled out, and while Morgen said everything, the tine just stood silent and solemn and made no reply. Then the questions died into silence and Morgen stared at the tine and the tine stared at Morgen, and Morgen's heart started beating because she wanted to know what was happening and the tine was so silent and solemn, she was afraid to ask any more.

Then the tine put his hands into the folds of his garments and brought out white clothes. They were made of a cloth that was softer than silk and unlike anything Morgen had seen in her life, sparkling and glowing and almost alive. Morgen couldn't take her eyes off the clothes. The tine offered them to Morgen, and she just couldn't move. She looked at the clothes a long time. Then she looked at the tine. Then she put out her hands and the tine put the clothes in them.

'Put the clothes on,' said the tine. 'I will come back for you.' And the tine wrapped his covers around himself again and went away, through the window as he came, and away through the mist.

Morgen stood a long time with the clothes in her hands, gently touching them and turning them over and staring at them. It came into her head that she wouldn't wear the clothes, as the tine said that she should. She knew nothing about what was going on. She was still full of questions. Why should she be told what to do in this way? Why should these things all be happening to her?

Then it came to her, too, that the tines were good creatures, wise creatures, and she thought how they were like servants or friends of King Gerald, and only did good in the land. And without any more hesitation, she put the clothes on.

She was instantly changed. As she wrapped the white clothes round her body and as she felt their coolness and their softness and freshness for the first time, she trembled all over, and something had happened to her.

She forgot all about going home and the southern hill and mother and dad. And this really was a special day, more special than anything ever before, and she could hear very distantly the sound of the land preparing itself for something to happen, and she prepared herself too. She took the white veil and placed it upon her head, right over her hair. Outside, everything was still covered in the thick, pale mist. Inside, Morgen was covered as well, and she was like a new flower with new petals before they are opened. And as soon as she had finished her dressing, a calmness came to her as never before.

She went to the window and waited for the tine to come back. She sat very patiently with the new calmness upon her. And the tine did come back. He saw that she was ready and he looked very gently at her and seemed moved by the sight of her, and he took her hand and together they passed through the window and out into the white mist.

Morgen could see nothing at all, but the tine seemed to see everything and she was safe with her guide. And although it was a cold morning and although it was damp with the mist all around, and although Morgen's wonderful new clothing was flimsy and thin and without such essentials as shoes and warm coverings, Morgen was not cold, nor did she suffer any other discomfort.

It soon became apparent that they were on the upward slopes of some hill. Morgen thought that this could not be possible because they were in the town and there just weren't any hills in the town, or around it. But Morgen could feel grass underneath her feet and the mist began to ease as they went on up and she could begin to make out the shapes of the trees and the lines of the fences and hedges around the edges of fields. And as they passed under the big, old trees, drops of dew that had gathered on the undersides of branches winked and sparkled at them, and wet spiders' webs gleamed and smiled, and Morgen knew that they were in some country place, and she could not understand how this could possibly be.

The walk became quite steep, but Morgen was not tired at all. Gradually, everything was becoming light and clear and there was the sun above them, on the other side of the mist. And then, quite suddenly, they were on the other side of the mist, and only the fresh air lay between them and the sun, and Morgen could see everything plainly.

Morgen and the old tine were near the top of the hill now, and they were walking across a meadow that was full of buttercups and long grass. Beneath them, the mist folded up into itself like a big, soft ball, and it disappeared right away, and then Morgen could see the things below, all the little divisions between fields, and the animals grazing and the villages and the orchards and the wooded areas and the country people moving about in the lanes. And in the same way that the mist had been extraordinary and strange and everything else had been extraordinary and strange, so the new scenery was strange, for everything was clearer and crisper and brighter and fresher than anything ever before. And Morgen, who had heard the land preparing itself for the day, could see, now that the mist had gone, what a wonderful job it had done. For the whole land seemed quite changed.

There was one other thing that Morgen took in. It took hold of her attention and gripped her. For she knew all the fields and the orchards and the villages and the wooded areas and the places where the animals grazed. The sight was very familiar and pleasing and lovely. Spread out beneath her was the big, wide valley that she knew from her childhood, and the dark hill stood in the distance, and the wild wood next to it, and she stood on the southern hill pasture. Morgen was home.

But she didn't go rushing down through the pastures and through the orchards and into the place at the bottom of the southern hill where mother and dad would be found. For in the moment that she saw where she was, Morgen saw something else too.

The southern hill pasture was covered in cotties. Cotties sat in the long grass all around her. Cotties sat in the ditches along the edges of the fields. Cotties hung in the trees, cotties hung in the hedges. And the cotties were Morgen's friends from a long time ago, and her heart leapt to see them and it was almost as good as a second sun rising to brighten the day, and she let out a cry and turned round every way, and wherever she turned, there were even more cotties to be seen, and she thought it a festival day, and that was why she'd come in these clothes and that explained what was happening. And she laughed out aloud with the joy of it all and wanted to go running about to meet her old friends. And she was so excited and so thrilled with her homecoming that she didn't know which way to turn or what to do first, or even what she could say to express what she felt.

The tine took her hand very firmly and led her along to the higher part of the pasture. But Morgen's calm had melted away and she was bubbling with joy and excitement, and she poured out fresh questions which the tine would not answer. The tine walked very fast. Morgen caught up the ends of her clothes and half ran to keep up with his pace, and she spilled out her questions and the tine was still silent.

Then the fleetings came over. There was a sudden plague of light in the sky and Morgen looked up and the fleetings were there. The sky was full of them. The tine pulled his covers more safely around him because of the light, and made Morgen go faster. And Morgen went faster, laughing all the time and shouting out greetings to all her old friends. And the fleetings filled the sky, more and more of them, until there was hardly any blue or any sun. And the cotties filled the land.

They came to the top of the pasture and the ridge at the top of the southern hill. Then they stopped. Morgen stood there with the land all covered in cotties below her and the sky all covered with fleetings above her, and she felt like a queen, and she felt very gay and excited and ready for the feasting to begin, and ready for dancing and music and laughter and being with her friends once again.

The fleetings came out of the sky and down onto the land and joined with the cotties and they all sat on the ground and became very quiet. Morgen stood in her white clothes, all covered with dew and drying in the sun as the petals on flowers were drying in the pastures all around her. And she was itching for music and dancing and just nothing happened, and Morgen stood waiting and the creatures were silent and still.

Then Morgen looked at the land, and it had never been better in the whole of her life, and she breathed very deeply and there seemed to be so many things in the air, like the best of all seasons rolled into one, that she turned in surprise to the tine by her side.

'This is nothing,' said the tine, 'compared to what King Gerald will make of the land when he comes.'

Morgen heard his words and a fresh little feeling came to her that this wasn't a festival after all and that something else was happening. And the creatures heard his words too, and it was very, very quiet indeed, after he spoke. Morgen wanted the tine to say more, but the tine looked away and was silent.

Then a sound came gently into Morgen's ears. It was a soft, mellow sound and it came very faintly. It grew slowly stronger and all the creatures heard it and there was a stirring among them. The sound still came stronger and louder and closer. There were movements in the distance, pinpricks of life while on the southern hill all else was still. The sound grew louder and louder, stronger and stronger, the song of the westels, and the pinpricks came closer and closer, the westels on the march.

They crossed over the land in every direction, and they sang as they came. The water of their homes still clung to them and the sun shone upon them and they sparkled like jewels as they came. They came up the southern hill and their song came up with them and the creatures parted, this way and that way, to let them pass through, and the westels came close in a very great company. They stood like sweet children all around Morgen, shy of their loveliness, and shy of the creatures around them, and shy of the person before them, and they sang all the time.

There was nothing that Morgen could say. She could not even move. But she cried to see the westels there and she cried to hear their song, for she'd never seen such loveliness in the whole of her life and she'd never been so moved by a sound.

And while Morgen stood crying, the last of the creatures came among the great company. The tines came down from the high hills and out from the dark caves. They walked very slowly and they were all, to the very last one, wrapped about in great covers that protected them all from the sun. And they seemed very old as they came along the top ridge of the hill, moving slowly, and they seemed very proud as they pulled themselves upright and tall and as they took their place in the company.

The wise ones had come out from under the earth, and all

the creatures were there, all together at last. And when Morgen looked upon the wise ones who had faithfully kept the land's wisdom away from all danger, down in the darkness, and when she saw how proud and how tired they were, the tears froze in her eyes, and she became full of wonder.

When they were all gathered in their mighty assembly, the tine who had brought Morgen along to the hill turned towards her.

'You people are loved by the king more than any of us,' said the tine, 'and only you, of us all, cannot see what is happening.'

He smiled gently, and all the creatures smiled gently, and the westels parted and the fleetings passed through and came up to Morgen. They brushed across her face and her arms with their wings, very softly, and when they had finished they went back again to the company. Then the old tine nodded to himself and he rearranged Morgen's veil and turned her head upward.

'King Gerald is coming,' he said. 'King Gerald is coming.'

And he went right away from her and joined the assembly, and she stood on her own on the top of the hill.

The westels suddenly started singing a new song, a strange song. And one by one, the other creatures joined in and they sang raggedly behind the westels until all their voices reached right up to the blue of the sky and echoed round it and came down again, and spread over the land.

But Morgen did not sing with the creatures. King Gerald, whom people had loved without seeing, was coming. King Gerald was coming. She remembered the times she had asked the creatures to tell her what King Gerald was like, because they had seen him. And now she would see him as well.

Then the old tine stepped out on his own.

'This is the time,' he shouted out loudly above all the din of the song. 'King Gerald returns to us.'

The creatures were suddenly silent. The birds stopped their singing. The wind stopped its noise in the trees. Everything stopped.

The old tine suddenly turned into something that resembled a flame, but pure white and splendid as no flame had ever been before, and then he became a tine again. And the whole sky opened up, like the lid of a box, and light came flooding in from outside, wonderful light that seemed so new that it made the best of everything else that had ever been good seem stale and old and used.

The light came into Morgen and it came into the old tine and it came into all the other creatures and they could see and feel and know nothing but the light that had come into them. The tines threw down their covers and were no longer afraid of a land full of light. The westels glowed. The fleetings glowed. The cotties glowed. And Morgen in her white clothes was glowing too. And a wonderful stillness came among them all, and they all stood waiting.

Then, in the moment of waiting, and in the stillness and peace, and while everything upon the southern hill stood still, all over the land something happened. The sleepers in their graves awoke. Esther awoke. Old Lovepace awoke. The miller's wife Maud awoke. Basketweaver and Old Woman awoke. Kerry awoke. Many, many other people awoke and Little Hoe awoke like the father of them all. And while time stood still on the southern hill and all the land stood waiting, the dead who had loved the king and died loving him greeted each other and rejoiced and made music and danced with great glee and ran in and out of the houses full of joy that the time had at last come to them. And they drew all the time to the southern hill and the wild wood, and they felt new life flooding through their bodies as they went on their way.

Then something happened to these people, and it happened to Morgen on the top of the southern hill as well. It was as though a hand came down through the blue of the sky and plucked her up through it. And the hand was King Gerald, and Morgen stood all in white, like a bride in his hand. And she met with King Gerald, and the other people met with King Gerald, while the land far beneath them stood waiting. And secret things happened when they met with the king at the top of the sky, and these things will never be spoken about. But the joy of the people was great and beyond our understanding.

Then King Gerald came down through the sky, and his

palace came with him, and the people came with him as well, and in the stillness and light, the moment of waiting was over for the creatures and King Gerald returned to his land.

The sky folded back and the palace came down and as it came, slowly, the things that it passed were restored from their spoiling. The palace rested at last in the wild wood by the waterfall, and in that instant the restoration was completed. Dead things were made alive and sorrow was replaced by joy and wickedness was driven right away. Every little thing in nature, from the smallest flower to the greatest tree, from the smallest animals to the greatest, was changed. And not slightly either, but the difference was as much as that between life and death. For to all in the land, and the creatures as well, a glory was given, and everything shone with the glory.

But the glory of King Gerald was beyond all these things. He was the light that gave light to all things, and the life too, that gave things their life and their glory. And the creatures in their company turned to the place where his palace had rested. They passed along the southern hill singing loudly a song for the king, and as they passed through the land, the land sang as well.

Now King Gerald was in his palace and the people were with him. And as everything else had changed and been given a glory, so the people were changed from before. They were beautiful and strong, and stood in white clothes that were softer than silk, with their heads covered over, and Morgen among them, and she was the flower fully opened at last, and they all were like flowers fully opened, glowing and happy and very fine and very fair, with King Gerald, whom they had loved without seeing, in the midst of them all.

And King Gerald himself was very full at the sight of them all, and very moved. He took them all out to a terrace along the side of the palace. The trees of the wild wood hung all around and the little streams crossed at the foot of the valley and the waterfall tumbled into a pool. A silver tree was growing on the terrace, and underneath its branches, and set out all around it and spread out in splen-

dour, was the most magnificent feast that has ever been seen.

'This is our feast,' said King Gerald, and he looked at the people with joy in his eyes at the sight of them there. 'It is the feast of the king and his people.'

He listened very carefully, and he could hear the songs of the land and the songs of the creatures as they danced their way down through the wood.

'Let us go to our guests,' said King Gerald to the people. 'Let us go out and greet them.'

And he took the people through the palace, under the columns of stone, set all about with fine stones and with silver, and the pillars of marble and the courtyards and the little palace gardens and the fountains, and across the great flagstones which were made of pure gold. And all through this journey, the songs of the creatures grew stronger and louder as they came to the palace.

Then King Gerald and the people came out of the palace, through its great doors of finely wrought gold and great pearls. And spread out in front of them was the happiest gathering you ever have seen.

The cotties were there at the front eager and smiling and joyful and rushing about as was always their way. And the westels were there, and their simple children's faces were shining with happiness. And the fleetings were there, like flowers tossed across the sky, like garlands of flowers. And the tines were there too, tall as ever, proud as ever, smiling like all the creatures, and crying with happiness as well, that the days in the darkness were over at last.

Now, when he stood before this great gathering, and when he saw that the gathering was complete, King Gerald spoke out. He brought the people around him and they stood all in white, and they shone like fair flowers in the morning. He drew the people to him, as he had drawn the land to him in the moment he returned. And he said to the gathering, 'This is a great mystery. The people have become my bride.'

Then a great peace came upon them all. The final and most wonderful mystery was taking place and the creatures marvelled to see it before them.

For the people stood with King Gerald in their white

clothes, with their heads covered over, and the land that had become perfect and lovely stood perfect and lovely and holding its breath and waiting around them. And in the quietness and goodness that surrounded them, King Gerald loved the people, and the people loved the king.

Twelve

CONCERNING A RICH MAN
AND A VERY SPECIAL JOURNEY

A rich man was going on a journey. He sat in a big, black car that was as high as a cathedral and as wide as the ocean itself, and he spread his body about and felt better than anyone else in the land. Life was so good. He read a paper for a while and then, when he became bored with the paper, he switched on the wireless and fiddled around trying to find an interesting programme. The little machine crackled about as he turned the knob from station to station, but nothing happened and in the end he gave up.

Having nothing better to do, the rich man looked out of the window. It was summer and the orchards which had been heavy with blossom were now heavy with a massive crop of fruit. The fruit meant more money for the rich man and he couldn't help but feel rather pleased with himself, almost as though he had made the blossom with his own hands and provided the country with the good, strong sun that was ripening it. For all the orchards, as far away as he could see, were the property of the rich man, and all the people in the orchards, and in fact everybody in that part of the land, was employed to take care of his property. And so it was that the rich man was very important in that part of the country.

The rich man thought, vaguely at first, that he had never seen the land looking so good. He had certainly never seen the promise of such a great crop of fruit. And he had never seen such green, fresh grass, nor such a bright, clear blue sky. The window of the big, black car was down and he could hear birdsong that was more beautiful than ever before and he could smell a sweetness about the earth that was quite different from anything that the earth had ever given up before. The rich man noticed all these things because he took delight in noticing good things in his land. It pleased him greatly that his land should have the best of everything.

He noticed as well, and his noticing was much less vague by this time, that the people he passed in the orchards and on the roads were as exceptional as the day was itself. They were in keeping, it seemed, with the mood of the day. For they were the finest people you could ever imagine. They were bright and very gay, and it seemed to the rich man that they looked happier and healthier than he'd ever seen people before. The rich man was pleased about this, of course, because they lived and they worked on his land. But he was beginning to grow just a little bit puzzled, about the day and the land and the people and why everything was so much better than ever before.

The rich man couldn't see any reason, you see, for the people to be as they were. They were lucky, of course, to have the privilege of working on his land. But that did not explain why they were ordinary yesterday and different today. They had worked on his land yesterday. And the rich man just could not believe that a single fine day could bring this about. For it seemed more as though these strong, happy people were taking part in some holiday, May Day or Midsummer, and the rich man almost expected them to come rushing up to his car to wave to him and shake his hand and call out their greetings, as was the custom on festive occasions.

But this was not May Day, nor was it Midsummer. It was not any feast day at all, and the people certainly took no notice of the rich man in his big, black car. It was an ordinary day of the week. The rich man had to remind himself of this several times. There was nothing special about the day, oh no, it was an ordinary day. The women should be busy in their houses or in the village. The children should be at school. And the men should be working.

The rich man realized, slowly, that nobody was doing what they were supposed to be doing at all. And he realized that he could not make an ordinary day of a special one, however hard he tried. The people in the orchards weren't working in them, they were just passing through. And those on the roads had no look of workers about them either. They were all heading in the one direction, the rich man in his car too, and at each corner and turning in the road, their numbers were added to. The land was full of people.

By now, the rich man had stopped feeling so pleased with life and so satisfied with himself. These people had taken a holiday! And it was a holiday without his authority, too! He had known nothing about what was going on, he still knew nothing about it. There was work to be done on the land, and without the work being done the crops would be wasted and the animals would be scattered and lost and the little industries, for the rich man had these too, would fail to make their profits and their failure would have to be paid for out of the rich man's own pocket.

He tapped the glass that separated him from the driver. But the driver seemed not to have noticed.

He tapped it again and shouted, 'I say, what's going on? Where are all these people going?'

The driver had a dark sort of face and he kept it right down and wouldn't show if he had heard what the rich man was saying. He began to drive a little faster, but he had nothing to say in reply to the rich man.

The rich man was very indignant. He was an important man in this part of the land, and he demanded respect from the people who worked for him.

'Did you hear what I said?' he demanded. 'I want to know what's going on. Why aren't those people at work? The work's still got to be done, even if the sun is shining. They can't just take holidays as they please, you know.'

The driver was looking down at the road. He increased the speed of the car and made no reply.

The rich man was suitably alarmed. Something was very wrong here and he couldn't understand it at all. It was as though magic was in the air and he was outside it. Or as though the whole of the land had been let into a secret and he was the only one left who hadn't been told.

While he was still thinking these things, the big, black car shot into the village, like a bullet hot from a gun. The streets were full of people. Some were running about from one side to the other, and others were just wandering along, not at all aimlessly, but without any awareness, it seemed, of the things all around them. Doors and windows were wide open and people shouted across to each other from balcony to balcony. Through the open window of the car, the rich man heard fiddle and flute and the sounds of dancing, and he knew that whether he'd approved it or not, the village was in the middle of some great festivity.

He was filled with rage. If the driver hadn't woken him up with a message about being wanted elsewhere, he wouldn't have left the house today. It seemed that the country people knew when he would be staying at home and took advantage of the fact that he kept apart from them. He wondered how often they'd danced and rejoiced and sung and played instruments when he had thought they were out taking care of his interests. And he was angry as well that his presence in the big, black car seemed not to affect them at all. They continued in whatever they were doing as though he wasn't there. There was no shame at being caught cheating him out of his due. None of them, indeed, took even the slightest notice of his presence. The rich man began to wonder about his standing with the country people. How dared they ignore him! Where was their shame?

He tapped the glass again, very smartly. 'Stop the car,' he demanded. 'I want to find out what's going on.'

But the driver took no notice, and the quiet cathedral of a car glided on, smooth as ever and faster than before. It seemed almost as though the rich man was master of nothing after all. The driver of the car it seemed was quite beyond control, and the things that were happening were far beyond the rich man's wildest imaginings. The beginnings of a very great fear crept into him.

A woman stepped out into the road. She was dressed in homely clothes, an apron tied round her waist and slippers on her feet. Her hands were covered with flour, as though she had just left the kitchen and come out into the street. Her cheeks were wet with tears and her eyes were bright and glorious. She stared straight at the big, black car, and she did not see it. She was an ordinary, motherly woman, but there was too much glory filling up her streaming eyes for her to see danger anywhere.

The rich man leaned out of the window and screamed at her, at the same instant shouting for the driver to stop. The driver, however, neither stopped nor swerved. He continued, straight on his path and if anything with greater speed, and for a terrible moment the woman was there and then the car was there and the woman was gone and the rich man was filled with horror and speechless with sickness. He turned and looked behind on the road, expecting to see her body lying crushed and dreadful and lonely, and he shook mightily with the expectation.

But the woman stood much as she had been. She had her arms around her body and she was swaying gently in tune with the breeze and she was singing loudly. After a moment or so, she was joined by other people, men and women and children as well, and like all the people, they turned in one direction and began to walk along the road.

Then the rich man was out of the village and in the lanes again. Only this time they were unfamiliar lanes. They were that part of the land that led down into the woods on the one hand and up to the hills on the other. The rich man didn't own the wild wood, nor did he own the hills, and he had never seen reason to go visiting such places.

He was still shaking from his experience in the village and he was as full of rage as ever, but the rage had lost its force because he now knew how little power he had any more. He directed his weak rage against the driver, demanding, at first in a quivering voice but later with what he supposed to be confidence, that the driver release him. He tried to make unpleasant threats. And in desperation he tried to open the door of the car in order to fling himself out. He counted any injury received in such an action as nothing compared to the danger of remaining for one minute more with the driver who would stop for nothing and listen to nothing.

But the door would not open, and when he tried the door on the other side of the car, that would not open either. And the driver would take no notice of anything the rich man said or did and the car would only roll along at a speed that grew more and more alarming.

The rich man looked about him in the lanes and he cried for help. But it was as though some magic thing had taken place, for the lanes that had been full of people just a moment before were suddenly empty and bare. The land was lovely as before, but the people were gone.

And now the driver took the big, black car and its passenger up into the beginnings of the hills, and he turned the car away from the good places and the places of sunlight, and began the long climb up the dark hill where nothing grew at all.

The rich man beat against the glass dividing wall between himself and the driver. The seeds of fear, well planted, were growing fruitful.

'What are you doing?' screamed the rich man. 'Answer me, answer me! Where are the people? Why won't you answer me when I speak to you? Where have the people gone? What's going on?'

The driver answered only by continuing on his way, speeding the car even faster, and starting to cut dangerously across corners in the road. Then the rich man realized that there was not even any other traffic on the road, and in the big, black car he was most terribly alone.

They were driving up into the dark hill. This place was cool and dim and quiet and the rich man was the prisoner of the man behind the wheel and he was in very great danger, more than anything he had ever known. He tried to be calm, but he was not calm at all.

'Please stop the car now!' he said, in an attempt to be restrained and civilized and reasonable.

Nothing stopped.

'I demand that you let me out,' said the rich man, trying to sound as though he was in control of the situation and of himself too. But he was not in control of anything, nor would he be, ever again. The driver continued on his crooked path, jumping across bends in the road and leaving great chasms beneath.

The rich man tried to believe that the driver had failed to hear anything he had said, but sometimes the driver softly laughed, and the rich man heard him laughing and he knew that all his demands had been heard, because the driver laughed like this.

Then he tried to believe that this was all a dream. After all, cars could not fly across chasms. He had never had reason to be afraid of his driver before. And the country people had never failed to greet him when he went out among them. And it was not possible to drive right over anybody and still leave them standing up and quite unharmed. And people didn't disappear into the air. But even as he thought these things, the rich man knew that this was not a dream. It was all too real to be a dream.

He scraped at the glass that separated him from the driver. He left soft, damp patches where his hands had been, and he noticed, for the first time, that he was wet with fear.

The driver took notice of the silent appeal. He pressed a button and the glass folded down, but he continued with his journey and he said not a word.

The rich man leaned forward. 'I beg you to stop,' he said. 'Take me home again. I'll make it worth your while. Just name something, go on, don't be afraid, anything you like from the house, or money if you'd rather have that. I promise it shall be yours.'

The driver said nothing, and the rich man ground his hands together in a rich man's gesture.

'I'll make you chief of my house,' he said. 'And leave you in charge of my estate. You shall manage all these things, just as you see fit, and employ who you like to help you.'

The driver's mouth was twisted by these words into amusement. The rich man caught the smile side on because the driver kept his head down and away from looking straight at him, and even sideways on, the smile was cold and ominous.

'Oh stop, stop, please stop!' implored the rich man. 'I give you my house. Take it and everything in it, but please stop.'

He expected some sort of reaction to such a generous offer. His house was very big, and there were many little treasures inside it. But the driver just continued, silent and amused.

'You can just leave me here,' said the rich man. 'Let me

out of the car and I'll find my own way out of the hills. You don't have to worry about taking me back or anything. Just let me out here.'

The driver showed a row of even little teeth and that was all. He seemed to avoid lifting his head and looking at the rich man eye to eye, even through the driver's mirror. He didn't seem to want to look at him at all.

The car sped on and the hill grew darker and it was bare and lonely. The wind was high and there was little vegetation, just rocks and some brown fern and tough, withered heather.

'All my possessions,' begged the rich man. 'Take them all, please take them. I've got industries and farms and orchards, and there's the estate and the house, I've said you can have that, and everything in the house, just like I said. Take them, please.'

He tried to reach out and touch the driver, but a pain came suddenly into him and he knew that the driver surely enough was surrounded by his own magic. He cried, and folded his body in around himself.

They were high on the hill now, and the air was grey and forlorn, and distantly from below, the song of the grass wailed as the wind rubbed up against it, tortuously and constantly.

'I'll work for you,' said the rich man, 'if you'll let me. If you'd like me to. I'll look after your lands, just as you please. I'll honour all your words and obey your commands. I'll be a good servant to you. Just let me out of this car so that I can get out of this terrible hill!'

The driver lifted his head and he looked at the rich man for the first time, through the driving mirror. He drove up the hill like a wild thing and one possessed. The rich man looked into the mirror, and shook at what he saw. For he was looking at two deep, dark spaces where eyes should have been. And the driver was still silent, but the spaces spoke words that went right into the rich man's head.

'Your fate is mine,' said the spaces where eyes should have been. 'Your end is mine as well.' And the words that the spaces were saying repeated themselves over and over again, and the rich man sat mesmerized and shaking all

154

over. He looked away, and the words seemed to stop. He was still shaking mightily, and when the words stopped it all seemed very silent around him.

Then the rich man offered the only thing left, the most precious thing of all. He offered his daughter to the driver, if he wanted her, as a wife.

'Take my daughter,' he said, 'and then you will have everything. Only leave me alone, and let me go!'

And he began whimpering, like an animal in pain.

And then the driver spoke out aloud. He had a soft, pleasant voice, and although the rich man would not have associated it with the fellow he knew as his driver, he did recognize in it the tones of an old friend, although he couldn't think who the friend might be. As he spoke, the driver smiled, and his words came out of his mouth and between clean, white teeth, as though they were spoken within him and not at all by his tongue and his throat.

'It is too late for these things.
The king has come to the valley and has made
   your riches into nothing.
Only one gift can you bring for me.
Only one thing can be mine for always.'

'Anything,' wept the rich man, and he was on his knees in his high, wide cathedral of a car, and his head was in his arms and his eyes were tightly closed for he was afraid to look at the cloudy hill any more. 'Just name that thing, and you shall have it.'

'That thing is yourself,' said the driver of the big black car.

'And that I already have.'

The rich man experienced the sinking of despair. 'What can I do?' he cried loudly. 'I don't understand what has happened. I don't understand what is going on in the land, what is happening to me and why the people disappeared and why they were so happy, or anything else.'

'Look behind,' said the driver.

But the places where his own eyes should have been remained fixed on the clouds that hid the tops of the hills.

The rich man looked back. The sun was shining on the

valley, on the little orchards and the fields. It was a happy scene. Once again, the rich man on the floor of his big, black car could sense the loveliness of summer, the freshest day of summer that had ever been. He could almost smell the sweetness of the earth and hear the richness of the bird-song and he was filled with a longing to be by the side of the road or in the fields and going wherever all the simple people had gone, and mixed up in their festivity.

The rich man looked up. The sky above the valley was bright blue and lovely. And it was full of magic people, clouds of creatures with great white wings, strung together like the flowers of a garland. And the top of the sky seemed to have opened up so that a new sort of light shone through it, and the new light filled everything, like the light of all the good things that people have striven for.

And then, through the top of the sky and very slowly down into the land, came a wonderful palace. And when the rich man saw the wonderful palace coming into the land, he knew what was happening at last, and he saw all things changed, as the palace passed by them.

For the rich man knew the king had come. He knew that his tears would continue for a long time, but they would be no more tears of fear. He knew that he would cry because he never would stand in the warmth of the new light, nor would he join with the people in their gladness, nor would he feast at the king's great feast. And he knew that he would always belong to whatever is bare and dark and sorrowful. He looked at the driver through the mirror at the front of the car. And the dark spaces where eyes should have been were looking at him and were saying, 'Your fate is mine. Your end is mine as well' over and over again, without ceasing.

At last the big, black car slowed down and stopped. The driver got out and moved round the side of it and opened the door. There was a horrible coldness and a terrible smell, the odour of desolation, and into all this stepped the rich man, quietly and grimly. Loneliness engulfed him like a cloud. He turned back and wished himself inside the frightening black car, chasing across chasms and along roads at the driver's dreadful pace. But when he looked back, the car had disappeared, and when he tried to look down into the valley, a great cloud came between him and the land, and he felt himself lifted up out of the land.

He wept bitterly. He was standing with a great company of men and women, and they all wept bitterly.